Family Planning

Also by Michael Z. Lewin

Family Planning

Michael Z. Lewin

Thomas Dunne Books
St. Martin's Minotaur
New York

THOMAS DUNNE BOOKS.
An imprint of St. Martin's Press.

FAMILY PLANNING. Copyright © 1999 by Michael Z. Lewin. All rights reserved. Printed in the United States of America. No part of this book may be used or reproduced in any manner whatsoever without written permission except in the case of brief quotations embodied in critical articles or reviews. For information, address St. Martin's Press, 175 Fifth Avenue, New York, N.Y. 10010.

Book design by Ellen R. Sasahara

Library of Congress Cataloging-in-Publication Data

Lewin, Michael Z.
   Family planning : a Lunghi family mystery /
Michael Lewin.—1st
  St. Martin's Minotaur ed.
  "Thomas Dunne books."
    p.   cm.
   ISBN 0-312-24391-X
   I. Title.
  PS3562.E929F38 1999   99-33280
  813'.54—dc21   CIP

First Edition: October 1999

10 9 8 7 6 5 4 3 2 1

For Roger and Liz, with love

Acknowledgments

Many people helped as I wrote this book but I'd particularly like to thank: Luigi Violino (who, with his wife, runs the wonderful La Bisalta restaurant in Frome, near Bath), for his assistance with Italian and pasta; Mariko Fujii, whose stories about her children I pinched; and Henry Kahn, who put me within spitting distance of knowing what I was talking about.

1

*A*ngelo was clearing the breakfast dishes when he heard the Old Man on his way down the stairs from the flat above. He turned to the kettle and filled it with water.

The Old Man rarely agreed to tea that he knew was being made specially for him. But chances were the Old Man wouldn't notice what his son was doing. Chances were he would come in and talk about what was on his mind, and by then the tea would be ready to pour. But even if the Old Man did notice, Angelo would say, "I was making it for myself."

The pot was still warm so Angelo spooned in loose tea leaves. Then he turned to the door. But what he heard was the Old Man cross the landing and begin to descend the stairs to the street. No hello, no tea, no nothing.

"Papa?" Angelo called. "Papa?"

The footsteps on the stairs continued, unchecked.

Angelo heard his father arrive at the bottom, open the door, step out, and close the door behind him.

The water in the kettle came to a boil. Angelo ignored it.

No law said that his father couldn't go out without stopping for a morning chat and a cuppa. There was not even a law that said that the Old Man had to respond when spoken to. But unresponsiveness was, to put it mildly, not his father's style. Puzzling.

Gina stood at the window overlooking Walcot Street when Angelo arrived in the office. She was watering the plants.

"The post is on your desk," she said. "The only message on the machine that might qualify as important was from Tarquin at Oglivy and Walls. He says the check is in the post."

Gina expected Angelo to comment on the message or react to hearing the name "Tarquin" again. Instead Angelo asked, "What's up with Papa?"

"Up?"

"Papa came down the stairs, didn't even open the door to say he wasn't coming in. Then I called to him and he didn't answer."

"Oh," Gina said. Such a thing was unusual. Yet there might be any of a number of explanations. Mightn't there?

"I haven't done anything to get up his nose, have I?" Angelo asked.

"Not that I know of, but the week is young."

"Mmmm."

It seemed that Angelo wasn't feeling playful. But Papa's not stopping wasn't that big a deal, surely. "Maybe he was just preoccupied."

"With what? And where would he be going at this time in the morning?"

Gina shrugged.

"He isn't going deaf, is he?" Angelo asked.

"What?"

"Deaf."

"What?"

"All right, all right, all right."

"He hasn't seemed harder of hearing than usual," Gina said. "Except when he doesn't like what he's hearing."

"Do you think I should ask Mama?"

"Not at this point. Unless you're so worried that you won't be able to concentrate on work."

"Work? Oh," Angelo said. "So, what we got?"

"Nothing urgent, but there are a lot of things that will become urgent if they don't get done. And you've got the frock shop at noon."

"Ah."

"Make sure you get the right size," Gina said.

"What?"

"At the frock shop. Make sure to buy a dress that fits," Gina said slowly. "Honestly!" Whether the Old Man was preoccupied or not, his son certainly was.

Rosetta, Angelo's sister, appeared in the office at a quarter to one. She didn't start work until two—she did half days dealing with the detective agency's finances as well as other family business matters. The latter included everything to do with the tenants who rented the street-level shops below the Lunghi Detective Agency and the family flats. The Old Man's shrewd purchase long ago of adjoining buildings meant there was room for seven Lunghis in three generations to live alongside the agency. The only member of the immediate family to reside elsewhere was Salvatore, Rosetta and Angelo's elder brother. And Salvatore lived outside by choice, not necessity. His father had never adjusted to Salvatore's decision to become a painter and only do detective work when it suited him. His move out had done much to reduce family tensions.

Rosetta came into the office with a flourish.

"Half-switches," she announced. She stepped back on one foot and forward on the other, then returned them to their original positions, forward foot first. Then she did the same thing but with the opposite feet. "Half-switches!"

Gina looked up from her screen and smiled.

"Do you want to see a replay?" Rosetta asked. Line dancing now loomed large in Rosetta's life. She was sure that learning complex step sequences was making her normal movements more confident. And dancing meant she knew things that other family members didn't. And, no small thing, it had provided her with a new boyfriend. Christopher had not yet met the rest of the Lunghis. He worked many unsocial hours—nights and weekends—but his schedule was flexible enough to allow an increasing number of nights with Rosetta. Including Wednesday, when they went line dancing.

"Show me," Gina said.

Rosetta executed right and left half-switches again. "Ready for lunch?" The two women locked up the office and made their way through the corridors to the kitchen.

Mama and the Old Man lived in a separate flat upstairs. All the other Lunghis had rooms in what was technically Gina and Angelo's flat, a warren that stretched over three floors and across two buildings. Even Salvatore still had a room, although he never used it. Most of his space was used for storage and the bed for occasional guests.

Gina got things out of the fridge. Rosetta assembled plates and utensils to make sandwiches with. But as Gina put bread on the bread board, she stopped and looked at her sister-in-law.

"What?" Rosetta asked.

"You look happy."

"Do I?" But it wasn't a real question, and Rosetta's tone of voice served as its own answer. She *was* happy. Happier than she had been for ages.

"How is Christopher?"

Rosetta expected this question and had planned to answer it coolly. Fine, fine, she would say, how's Angelo? But although Rosetta said, "Fine; oh, fine," she heard the excitement in her voice. Rosetta stifled a giggle—that would be too much, just too childish. But then she blushed. Oh no. She felt it happening and saw that Gina saw it happening.

Rosetta tried to think of a way to escape her cardiovascular system. But was it better to ask about work and whether Angelo was out, or to say she was hungry and eager to eat? What Rosetta did say was, "Is Angelo lunch? Oh!"

Angelo sat in an armless, hard-backed chair. Beside him a woman in her early forties examined herself in a full-length mirror. The woman looked at her image this way and then that. Angelo felt much too close to the mirror, but reluctantly he concluded that to move the chair elsewhere would be noticed and embarrassing.

He uncrossed and recrossed his legs and followed the woman's self-examination from the edge of his field of vision. The woman was certainly watchable—attractive, glamorous even. Were those the same things? No, he supposed not. But she was not ordinary looking. And she was putting a lot of care into the choice she was making.

Angelo did not know how one was meant to describe the garment the woman had tried on. It was a dress of course, but although he knew there were words to differentiate types of dresses, he didn't know what they were. It was like Laplanders, who supposedly had dozens of words for different kinds of snow. If you were interested enough in something, you could see differences other people couldn't.

Probably there were situations in which it would be good if he were able to report to a client, "And the subject tried on a cerise, staggalee dress with a silly-midoff collar and a dibber hem." Or whatever. But Angelo didn't know the language of dresses, and so there it was. He was not even sure what color cerise was. All he did know about the dress the woman was trying on was that it was expensive.

"I'm not sure, Celia," the woman said.

Celia Corman, who owned the small dress shop, said, "I know the color isn't one you usually consider, but it works. And it certainly shows off your figure without making it, you know . . ."

"Too in-your-face?" The woman looked at the mirror yet again. "Nah, Erik's not *that* short." The woman changed her pose. "But I see what you mean."

Angelo glanced at the woman and her figure, just for an instant, then dropped his eyes to his watch.

But the woman had caught him. "What do you think?" she said. She took a stance before him.

"What do *I* think?"

"You make it sound as if your wife never asks you that

question, poor darling. Doesn't she care?" The woman looked to the mirror. "Honest opinion."

"Well. Well, is it meant for a formal occasion?"

"To the extent an event with Princess Anne can ever truly be called formal."

"And are you there on your own behalf or are you there for someone else?"

The woman tilted her head and looked at Angelo, seeing him for the first time. "For my daughter."

"In the dress you have on, you are striking, stunning even. But is it your objective to stun or to support?"

"What an interesting and apposite question."

"Because how something looks is as much a matter of context as a matter of fabric and cut," Angelo said.

The woman studied herself in the mirror. This time the expression on her face was critical. "I'm going to try the other one again, Celia." The woman drew her lips together as if she'd pulled a drawstring inside them. She made her way to the changing rooms in the back of the shop, swinging her hips extravagantly.

Angelo rose and moved close enough to Celia Corman to whisper, "I'm sorry if I did something wrong."

"Not at all, Mr. Lunghi. The other dress is the better one. You said exactly the right thing."

"That's a relief," Angelo said, not that he could remember exactly what he had said. He looked at his watch.

Celia Corman said, "They should be here any minute. They arrived at one on Friday, and on Saturday, and again yesterday. And the last thing I need with Christmas coming is—"

A short woman of about thirty said, "I'm sorry to interrupt, but is there a second changing room I can use?" This woman held two dresses on hangers.

Celia Corman spun on the spot. "Of course. I'll show you." She walked past the woman, pausing only to touch one of the dresses. "I love the feel of those. I have one myself, but in blue. And I can't tell you how sensual it feels next to my skin."

Angelo swallowed. He sat down. He looked at his watch. As he did, four women entered the shop. They were of assorted sizes, shapes, and hair colors. But all were young and they all had dirty faces. And they all wore what Angelo would describe as rags, unless there was some fashion term that he didn't know about for dirty clothes with holes. But even if there was, he doubted that there was a special fashion word for the mucus that hung from the noses of two of the young women.

The Old Man made his way slowly up the stairs. Fine, fine, fine, he thought, if you like that kind of thing. But so small at the front, compared to so big at the back. And what use could you make of upstairs?

The Old Man knew about buildings, about shops, if anybody cared to ask him. Maybe he didn't know so much nowadays about rentals, but look at the buys he'd made in his time. And those were rented first, and nobody was complaining. But fine. It was not for him to interfere. Interference was for Mama. An international-class interferer. Her only problem was which country to represent. England or Italy, which to interfere for.

The Old Man smiled to himself. She wouldn't like what

he said about interfering. But it *was* her speciality, no question, like lasagna for others. Ask Salvatore. Ask Rosetta. You want interference, go to Mama. *That* she should market. *That* she should open a business in.

As he reached the landing, the Old Man heard voices in the kitchen. He pushed through the door.

Gina and Rosetta both turned and smiled and said, "Hello, Papa."

Smiling faces. Friendly greeting, how it ought to be. Good girls, these. "I'm not interfering, I hope."

"I was just making us a fresh pot of tea, Papa," Gina said. "Sit down."

Rosetta pulled out a chair and the Old Man sat. He looked at his watch. "Quarter to two. You have time?"

"Of course," Gina said.

"It's not busy in the office?" the Old Man asked. "Business is bad?"

"Things are quiet, but not noiseless, Papa," Gina said. "And we got a new case this morning."

"What is it?" the Old Man said. "A husband doubts his wife? Maybe she's acting funny?" He smiled to himself.

"It's not that kind of case, Papa," Rosetta said.

The Old Man turned to Rosetta. A dim memory flickered. Didn't Rosetta used to have a husband? Not her own, someone else's. Yes, she brought a man to dinners. A married man with a wife. "So, what kind of case? A wife who doubts her husband?"

"It's extortion," Rosetta said brightly.

"We don't know exactly what it's about yet," Gina said. "Angelo's there now."

"Extortion?" The Old Man shook his head. "Extortions,

if the extortee pays out too much, then he can run out of money to pay the bills."

"Papa, are you and Mama coming to dinner tonight?" Gina asked.

"To dinner? Of course we come to dinner. It's Tuesday."

"Good. Then Angelo can tell us all about the case while we eat."

When Angelo came back to the office in the middle of the afternoon, he was eager to tell Gina about the "extortion" case. But no sooner had they settled with cups of tea than the office doorbell rang. "You expecting somebody?" Angelo asked.

"No," Gina said.

The bulk of the agency's work was for lawyers and arranged by telephone, so new clients almost never came in off the street. The family had once discussed removing the plaque by the door that read LUNGHI DETECTIVE AGENCY, FIRST FLOOR to prevent nuisance callers. But the deciding factor was that the others thought it would upset Papa to take it down. Mama confirmed the sentiment later to Gina. "It's his history."

The bell rang again. Angelo rose and went to the new intercom. "Which button?" he asked Gina. But he didn't wait for an answer. He pushed a button and said, "Lunghi Detective Agency."

"I can read that for myself," a female voice said. "Just open the damn door, will you?"

Angelo glanced at Gina. She shrugged. Angelo pushed the button that released the lock at street level. Then he went to the landing outside the office to see who came in. To his astonishment it was the glamorous woman from the dress shop.

Sitting in front of her computer, Rosetta hummed "Money to Burn." The dance that went with the song was Smokin' Cowboy, and the most difficult thing about it were the steps Christopher called half-switches. And the fact that the dance's step sequence was unusually long. Nevertheless, she'd just about mastered it. Christopher was wonderfully patient, although the dances came easily to him. Patience was just one of his many virtues.

Rosetta got up from her seat and moved to the space before her desk. From the office down the hall she heard voices, including one she didn't recognize. For a moment Rosetta considered going to see what the woman was talking to Gina and Angelo about.

But instead she began to hum again. She touched her right heel on the floor, crossed it in front of her left calf, and touched it again on the floor, this time on the other side of her left foot. Practice makes perfect. Lots of little repetitions add up to a big dance. Christopher said so, so lots of little repetitions there would be.

"I'm being threatened," the woman said.

"Biscuit?" Angelo said.

The woman ignored him. "And I wasn't sure what to do about it until today in Celia's shop."

"Celia?" Gina asked.

"Celia Corman," Angelo said. "Owns the dress shop I went to this morning."

"Your husband helped me choose a dress for my daughter's big day, Mrs. Lunghi."

"He did?"

"All part of the service," Angelo said.

"I could see there was something about you, Mr. Lunghi," the woman said. "I took Celia aside and asked who you were, and when she said you're a private detective, it was as if you'd been heaven-sent. I don't have to look for trouble myself because you can do it for me, if you will. So here I am. And I hope you are a real 'Angel-o,' because I don't mind telling you, I'm scared shitless."

"Shitless how, exactly, Mrs. . . . ?" Angelo asked.

"I'm Esta Dumphy. Mrs. Esta Dumphy, but please call me Esta and don't call me Dumphy because what I hear is 'dumpy,' and I loathe being called that."

"And where do you live, Esta?" Gina asked.

"Blind Lane. Do you know it? North of Weston Park and halfway to nowhere."

"That's the RUH area, isn't it?" Angelo said.

"Your ability to make connections continues to impress me. You're a lucky woman, Mrs. Lunghi."

"So is your husband a doctor?" Gina asked.

"Erik is a shrink, based at the Royal United. Which makes Blind Lane jolly convenient for him, however robust a pain in the gluteus maximus it is for me."

"Do you work?"

"Not beyond entertaining and being charming."

"And going with your daughter to formal events where Princess Anne is," Angelo said.

"Indeed. That's quite a memory you have there. Susan is receiving a prize which will be presented by the Princess

Royal next week. She has a real brain, has my little girl. Just as well."

"Esta," Gina said, "how exactly are you being threatened?"

"With this." From her belt Esta unhooked a small, gray box.

"What's that?" Angelo asked.

"My pager."

2

$\mathcal{A}$t six-thirty David was draining pasta at the sink. Marie, his sister, sat at the kitchen table with arms across her chest. A large salad bowl sat in front of her. "As far as I'm concerned, this salad is tossed," Marie said.

"It can't be a surprise," Gina said.

Marie sat silently. It wasn't a surprise. It was only too predictable, because it involved the response of a *parent*.

"You know perfectly well that we don't like you to go out early on a family dinner night. And certainly not unless it's for something special."

"It *is* special, Mum," Marie said.

"You go over to Cassie's house every night, unless she comes here," Gina said. "What's special?"

Unfortunately the reason Marie wanted to go to Cassie's early was nothing she could tell her mother. "It'll save on your precious telephone bill," Marie whispered.

"What was that?" Gina turned from the cooker to face her daughter.

Behind Gina, David stuck his tongue out at Marie.

Marie took a breath. "What I said was if I don't see Cassie, I have to talk to her anyway, on the telephone line or on the fax line or on one of the mobiles, and either way it's a lot lot cheaper if we talk face-to-face."

"So you want to go to Cassie's as a favor to me, is that what you're saying?" Gina gave her head a shake and turned back to the sauce pot.

"*Either* is for between two things," David said.

Marie looked at her brother as if he had no right to speak and ought to know it. "What was that, squint-squelsh?"

"You listed three things," David said, "so you shouldn't have said '*either* way.' You're so ignorant."

"You're the one who's ignorant," Marie said. "And a runt to boot."

"You're so ignorant that—" But David interrupted himself. "I've been meaning to tell you, Mum, do you know what I saw Marie do last Saturday?"

Gina had been about to end the siblings' skirmish by decree, telling Marie that she must stay for dinner but she could leave before pudding *if* she didn't bully people to eat faster. However Gina delayed giving her judgment. She was interested to hear what David had to say.

Marie too was diverted by David's intervention. "What am I *supposed* to have done last Saturday, billiard brain?"

"I was in town Saturday morning," David said, "and when I got back, it was lunchtime and Marie was in the kitchen, and do you know what she was doing?"

Lunchtime? Marie thought back. Lunchtime was all right. He knows nothing.

"What?" Gina asked.

"She was making spaghetti for herself and Cassie."

"So what, idiot breath?" Marie said. "So I was making lunch for me and my friend. People eat lunch. Human beings, that is. Which must be why it was so shocking to you, nerd . . ." Marie had been about to say "nerd nuts," but she realized she didn't want to say "nuts" in front of her mother. Considering.

But the sobriquet "nerd" struck home unadorned. David's voice elevated slightly as he said, "I may be a nerd, but at least I know how to cook spaghetti. Mum, she put it raw into the pan with the tomato sauce."

Gina looked at Marie.

"So what? We were in a hurry."

"She's so ignorant she doesn't even know she's supposed to cook pasta in its own pan!" David was triumphant. "Poor man, that's what I say."

"Poor man?" Gina said.

"The poor man she marries who has to eat her cooking," David said.

"Well, that shows what you know, byte bonce, because I'm not getting married. I'm going to have a career. So there. Nyah, nyah, nyah."

"*That* just shows you're even stupider than I thought, because it means you're going to have eat your own cooking all the time. Yuck! Double yuck. Double yuck squared."

Marie sat next to her grandfather. "Eat up, Granddad."

"Marie," Gina warned.

"I only mean it's good for him to eat." Marie turned back

16

to her grandfather. "You look thinner, Granddad. Have you been losing weight?"

"Weight?" The Old Man looked down at himself. "If so, the losing can only be from worry."

Salvatore, the Old Man and Mama's oldest child, sat across the table from his father. Although Salvatore's flat was in the center of Bath, he usually attended the three "family" meals each week. He said, "I've been thinking that too, Papa. You look thinner."

Marie faced her mother with an expression intended to extract acknowledgment that urging her grandfather to eat had not been an attempt to make the time she could leave for Cassie's come quicker.

But Gina was watching her father-in-law as he said, "To you I look thinner?" to Salvatore.

"Yes, you do."

"Huh." The Old Man considered. Although Salvatore's decision to paint still rankled, the Old Man didn't doubt that his elder son had an eye for detail.

"So what are you worrying about, Papa?" Salvatore asked. "Or is it something you don't want to talk about *avant les enfants?*" He winked at his mother.

"That means 'in front of the children,' " David said to Marie.

"I knew that," Marie hissed.

"Please, Salvatore, don't get him started on worries," Mama said with a sigh. "If he starts complaining, who can stop him? It's a runaway train."

The Old Man did not like being called a train. But he also didn't like to be thought of as a complainer, though there was enough to complain about. He did not respond to his wife. Instead he glared at her, took a forkful of food, and said, "Huh!"

"So, Angelo," Mama said, "Gina says you have a pager case."

"I heard extortion," the Old Man said. He turned to Rosetta, who nodded. "But talk about pagers. Go on. Would I complain?"

"We started two new cases today," Angelo said. "Which would you like, Mama?"

"I must choose?" Mama said. "We don't have time for both?"

Marie held her face in her hands.

"I meant, which would you like to hear about first?"

"Sounds like you had a busy day, bruvva," Salvatore said.

"What did he say, 'bruvva'?" the Old Man whispered to Mama. "It means something? Not that I'm complaining."

"He's being funny," Mama said. "His humor."

"The pager. Everyone knows what a pager is?" When no one sought explanation, Angelo said, "Well, today we had a woman who is receiving threats on her pager."

"Threats?" Salvatore said. "Like messages saying, 'I'm going to kill you'?"

Angelo raised a finger. "The woman's pager only receives numbers."

"Not messages?"

"Just numbers." Angelo spread his hands to invite everyone at the table to consider how someone could receive threats on a pager that only received numbers.

"Somebody throws her pager at her?" David suggested.

"Jerk bonce," Marie muttered.

"Nothing like that," Angelo said. "It's the numbers she receives on it."

There was a silence. Nobody had a suggestion.

"Okay," Salvatore said. "Tell us."

"Nine nine nine," Gina said. "Somebody pages her and leaves the number nine nine nine."

"She gets nine nine nine on her pager?" the Old Man said. "Emergency services?"

"That's right, Papa," Gina said.

"So what threat?"

"She takes it as somebody telling her she's going to need the police or an ambulance or firefighters."

"Huh," the Old Man said. "Not friendly, that I can see."

"And she's been getting the nine-nine-nine message for more than two weeks, sometimes four times a day," Gina said. "And she doesn't like it."

"Can you one-four-seven-one a pager message to see who's calling it in?" David asked.

"Good idea," Angelo said. "But we checked, and pager messages come through a service center. Tomorrow we're talking to the manager to see if there's some other way they can tell where the initiating calls are coming from."

"Any self-respecting threatener would dial one-four-one first to hide the number he's calling from," Marie said.

"Or she," David said.

"It's only males who make stupid threats," Marie said. "Especially *boys.*"

"Stupid or otherwise," Gina said, "our client finds them upsetting."

"She can pay, this woman?" the Old Man asked. "How does she come to us?"

"I met her in a dress shop," Angelo said. "An expensive shop, where she bought a dress. I'm sure she can pay, Papa."

"What were you doing in a boutique, bruvva?" Salvatore asked. "Or is that *pas avant les femmes.*"

"That's—" David said.

"I *know,*" Marie said.

"What then?" David asked.

"Hush, both of you," Gina said.

Marie stuck her tongue out at her brother.

"I was at the dress shop because of the other case that began today," Angelo said.

"The extortion?" the Old Man said.

"You tell me if it's extortion, Papa. What happens is that four young women come into a dress shop. But these young women are not customers. They are dressed in rags."

"Rags?" Mama said. "They're poor girls?"

"Actually their clothes looked pretty new to me, Mama, but torn up. Underneath there were more layers, so I don't think they were cold. But on top, everything you can see, it was all dirty and full of holes."

"Street chic," Marie said.

"What?" Angelo said.

"It's a style. Street chic."

"Does that include having dirty faces, and stuff dripping from your nose?" Angelo said. "And smelling bad?"

Salvatore said, "So what do they do in this boutique?"

"They stand together, near the door, not touching anything, not obstructing anyone, not saying anything. And," Angelo said, "they stay there."

"They stay in the shop and do nothing?" Mama said.

"In shops she has a sudden interest," the Old Man said. "Not that I would complain."

"That's right, Mama," Angelo said. "They stay there, until the shop owner offers them money to leave. Then they say, 'Thank you very much. See you tomorrow.' So, Papa, tell me. Is that extortion?"

3

*A*fter dinner was finished and the dishes put to wash, Gina and Mama sat at the kitchen table with cups of coffee. Marie had been released to visit Cassie. Mama asked, "Do you have any *palmier?*"

"No," Gina said, "but I have some *biscotti.*"

"Okay, good," Mama said. "Thank you."

As Gina got the biscuits out, she said, "I wanted to ask you, is Papa all right?"

"What? The thinner?"

"Angelo called to Papa as he went out this morning and Papa didn't answer."

"Ah."

"I wondered if maybe he's becoming hard of hearing."

"He hears if he wants to hear," Mama said, "but the rest is very hard, that's true."

"Mama?" Gina was picking something up.

"What?"

"Tell me."

"I . . . It's early yet, not settled." Mama dipped a biscuit in her coffee and then sucked on it. "This is how flavored coffee started. I'm sure."

Mama was entitled to have secrets. In fact, Gina was re-assured to know that something *was* going on, something of sufficient significance to make Papa go off his food, and to distract him. Whatever it might be. Gina dipped and sucked one of the *biscotti* too. If Mama didn't want to say, that was fine. Her business.

"It's not settled," Mama said again, "and it might not happen. So I would appreciate you don't mention it, but I am opening a restaurant."

"You're what?"

"Not by myself. It's Gabriella really." Gabriella was Mama's oldest friend. Both women had come to England from the same Piedmontese village.

"Even so," Gina said, "a restaurant?" Gina's own parents ran restaurants in Birmingham.

"Gabriella wants it, for her little Nina and the husband, for them to run the business. Gabriella and me, we'll help at the beginning, and with the money. And not such a big amount. Because it won't be a big restaurant, only small. They have a place in mind. And that's what Papa went to look at this morning."

"Oh," Gina said, though she didn't understand at all why Mama would suddenly want to take part in such a project.

"So," Mama said, "that's what's wrong with *him*. He doesn't like it. He thinks I throw money away and he thinks I won't take such care of him. But he's spoiled. He'll live."

"I daresay."

"So, Gina, there was something else wrong I wanted to ask."

"What?"

"What's wrong with Salvatore?"

"Wrong with Sally?" Such a notion hadn't crossed Gina's mind. Her brother-in-law certainly wasn't losing weight. And he seemed cheerful.

"You haven't noticed?"

"He seems the same as ever to me."

"Well the same he's not." Mama sat back in her chair and crossed her arms.

Gina searched her mind again, but she still couldn't find what Mama was getting at.

"So tell me," Mama said, "when was the last time he brought a woman to eat with us?"

"Oh."

"Oh? *Oh?* 'Models' he used to bring. And others. So where are they? Because if he brings them, if he goes out with them, at least there is a chance he'll settle. But, Gina, the last woman he brought was that Lisa on August Bank Holiday Sunday. Not ideal, but a nice enough little thing. And now today it is December second. Work it out for yourself. More than three months and nobody with him tonight again. Never has it been so long. Never. I'm so worried, it's me should be losing the weight." Mama took another biscuit.

The four men of the family sat at the dining room table. "So, bruvva," Salvatore asked, "what plan of campaign do you have in mind for your Dirty Girls?"

Angelo sipped from a bottle of beer. "I thought you could deal with them. There are only four. It's not likely to put a strain on you."

"Thanks," Salvatore said, "but I don't like them dirty."

"Dirty shows no self-respect," the Old Man said. "Dirty shows they could get up to anything."

"Good point, Papa," Salvatore said. "Where did you say I could find them again?"

The brothers laughed. The Old Man didn't understand why. He said, "How old are these Dirty Girls?"

"I would guess about twenty," Angelo said. "Might be younger."

"Old enough to know better," the Old Man said.

"Pity," Salvatore said.

"In the morning I need to confirm the law about what they're doing," Angelo said.

"Are you going to ask Charlie, Dad?" David asked. Charlie was the longest-standing of the family's contacts in the Bath police.

"The law?" the Old Man said. "A lawyer is obvious."

"I'll start with Charlie," Angelo said. "The real law will be more useful than the theoretical law."

"What's real law, Dad?"

"Real law is law that the police will enforce. That's not necessarily the same thing as what's written down."

"Charlie will advise for free," the Old Man said.

"There's that too," Angelo said.

"And this client, the dress owner, how much does she pay to get rid of these Dirty Girls?" the Old Man asked.

"It will depend how much work we do, Papa," Angelo said.

"What am I? Stupid? I don't need to be told that," the Old Man said. "How much does the dress shop pay out each time, to send them away? And how much more will she pay? Because extortion, if you pay you just have to pay again, and it can happen that you run out of money before you pay your bills. And who pays us then?"

"She's been paying them five pounds, Papa."

"Five quid a day?" David said. "That's not so much."

"Every day since Friday," Angelo said.

"So how did it start?" Salvatore asked. "They came in on Friday and asked for the money?"

"They never ask," Angelo said. "I established that specifically. They came into the shop—last Friday—and they stood inside the door, not touching anything, not getting in anybody's way. Finally Mrs. Corman asked them to leave."

"And?" Salvatore asked.

"They left, but they hung around on the pavement near the front door, which is as bad for business as if they were inside. And eventually it was Mrs. Corman who said, 'If I give you five pounds, will you go away?' The leader said, 'Sure,' so Mrs. Corman gave them the fiver and they left."

"She shouldn't pay," the Old Man said.

"When they came back again on the Saturday, she called the police. A bobby came around and asked the Dirty Girls to go. They did, but they came back ten minutes later. Mrs. Corman realized that the most the police could do would be to post someone at her door full-time, but a copper on the premises would hardly be better for business than the Dirty Girls. And," Angelo said, "with Christmas only a little more than three weeks away, Mrs. Corman doesn't want to take the chance that their price will stay at a fiver. These girls really are repulsive, Papa. I wouldn't want to go into a shop if I saw them there."

"I should talk to this Corman," the Old Man said. "Tell her not to pay."

"How about talking to the Dirty Girls?" David said.

"I did," Angelo said. "They just went outside when I asked them to."

"No, I mean talk to them," David said. "Find out who they are. If they're that poor, maybe you could find somebody to help them so they don't need to do the extortion."

Salvatore looked at Angelo. "Can't hurt to find out who they are, bruvva."

Angelo nodded in agreement. "Good suggestion, Son."

"As a reward," Salvatore said, "your father will let you have a swig of his beer."

"Thanks, Uncle Sal." David looked to his father.

Angelo passed his glass and David drank and choked and drank again.

"One swig," Salvatore said.

"Tell the Corman not to pay," the Old Man said. "Talk to *her.*"

Cassie passed Marie the cigarette. Marie made the end glow and then blew the smoke out Cassie's open window. The cold wind blew it back in. Marie waved at the smoke with her free hand.

"I think you should do it," Cassie said.

"Yeah?"

"You want to, right? And he wants you to. So, why not? You're only young once."

"So what about you?"

"I'll do it if you will," Cassie said, "assuming he's got enough for both of us."

The girls put hands over their mouths so that Cassie's

mother didn't hear their giggles and come in to ask what kind of homework they thought they were doing.

Cassie said, "But I don't particularly want to go all the way to Bristol. I don't see why we can't do it here."

"Going to Bristol is the good part for me," Marie said.

"Apart from the money."

"Apart from the money, of course. But if I'm in Bristol, there's less chance of getting caught."

"We're not going to get caught," Cassie said.

Marie considered. If there was one lesson to be learned from growing up in a house full of detectives, it was that the unlikely does sometimes happen. Still . . . "I would hate it if I got caught. My parents would go mental, absolutely mental. George has done time."

"My mum wouldn't like it much either," Cassie said, "but she'd keep it from my dad, because he'd say it was evidence she wasn't being a good parent, or some shit like that."

Cassie offered Marie the cigarette, but Marie shook her head and looked at her watch.

"Anyway," Cassie said, "I think you'll be better at it than I will."

"Me? Why?"

"You're more . . . outgoing than I am." Both girls giggled again because it was a reference to the state of development of Marie's chest.

There was a bang on Cassie's door. Cassie's mother called, "They didn't assign funny homework in my day."

Cassie choked and coughed. She dropped the cigarette on the floor. "Oops." She scrambled to pick it up and dust away the ashes.

"What a dirty girl you are!" Marie whispered.

. . .

From the bed Gina said, "In the morning it's what?"

Angelo stood at the wardrobe, trying to decide which trousers would go best with the shirt that already rested on the chair by his night table. "To see Charlie. I called. He's on duty all day."

"I'll make some calls about the pager, to see if they can trace calls."

"What time is the pager's appointment?"

"She said she'd be here at quarter past two."

Angelo picked trousers and moved their hanger to the end of the bar. "I'll serve some papers after Charlie, if there's time. Otherwise it's straight to the dress shop. I want to talk to Mrs. Corman before the Dirty Girls show up."

"To tell her what Charlie had to say?"

"And ask if she'll authorize me to follow when they leave."

"Why follow them?"

"To find out who they are, why they are doing this. It was David's idea." Angelo sat on the bed and took off his slippers.

"What if you follow and the Dirty Girls separate?"

Angelo picked at fluff between his toes. "Pick the cutest, I suppose."

"And get arrested for stalking?"

"Something like that." Angelo slid into bed.

"Do you want me to come out in case they separate?"

"You need to be here for the pager."

"I could call Salvatore. And Papa too, maybe?"

"I don't know if Corman can afford that."

"Or even you to follow," Gina said.

29

"True."

"What do you do about the Dirty Girls if she doesn't want to pay for you to follow?"

"Ah," Angelo said. "Then I move on to Plan B."

"Which is?"

"To draw up another plan."

There was a silence. Then Gina turned to her husband. "Speaking of Salvatore . . ."

In his room David left his computer. Four juggling balls rested on his bedspread. He picked up three and began to juggle. The pattern, called a cascade, sent each ball from one hand to the other and then back again.

David juggled the balls over his bed so that if he dropped one, he wouldn't make enough noise to disturb anyone. Gradually he varied the size of his cascade, making the path the balls took higher, then lower.

Then he worked with the two balls in just his right hand. He tried to throw them in steep loops, so that the ball going up didn't collide with the ball that was coming down.

He transferred the two balls to his left hand. He was worse with his left hand, so he practiced longer. Eventually, he hoped, he would be able to juggle four balls at the same time, two in each hand. He was not close to being able to do this yet, but he had already come a long way since Lena Taylor first showed him how to juggle.

Ah, Lena. Two years older she might be, but he could dream.

David's left arm became tired. He let the balls fall onto his bed and went back to his computer. He hit a few keys and brought up the Lunghi Detective Agency's case files. On the screen a message asked him to enter a security password.

In retrospect, he felt stupid to have taken so long to guess such an obvious word. That's what the hacker guides said, people use obvious words for security systems so they won't forget them. And for this system it had to be a word which his father, mother, *and* Auntie Rose wouldn't forget. Confidently David tapped out the word, *family.*

Inside the system David went to the active cases that were not just ongoing routine files for law firms and other regular agency customers. He didn't remember the name of the Dirty Girls client, but he thought he would recognize it if he saw it. And he did, "Corman."

He opened the file and read his father's summary of the case so far. He was disappointed to see that the Dirty Girls' arrival time at Mrs. Corman's was one. It would only be possible for David to get a look at these Dirty Girls if he cut school at lunchtime.

He leaned back and thought about his school timetable on Wednesdays. The last morning class was Maths. Then in the afternoon it was French and Activities.

Maths was no problem, but French he didn't find so easy. Still, Lena was doing French and he could ask her for help. Hmmm.

David wrote down the address of the dress shop and then closed the file. He exited from the family system and in its place on the screen he brought up a file of his own, which he had created by scanning into the computer the note his mother gave him so he could leave school to get to his real dental appointment. He printed a copy and then typed a new note laid out in exactly the same way. He printed this too.

He was about to trace his mother's signature when he wondered if the school secretary would notice that Gina's signature was exactly the same as last time. Should he try to vary it a little? Hmmm.

4

$\mathcal{A}$s Angelo walked to the police station through the city center, he became increasingly aware of the way everywhere was bursting with people—on the pavements, in cars, in shops. All right, it was Christmas. Or, to be more exact, pre-Christmas, a major get-out-of-the-house time of year. But could there possibly be anybody left who was *in* the houses, or schools or factories? If people weren't wearing heavy coats, you'd think it was Bath at the height of the tourist season.

He crossed Orange Grove, passed the subterranean public conveniences someone once tried to turn into a nightclub, and walked into Pierrepont Street. Art books in a window display caught his eye. They reminded him to think about Salvatore. *Was* anything wrong with his older brother?

Angelo went back through recent meetings with Sally. Certainly nothing seemed wrong with his bruvva's health. If anything, he looked better and moved more energetically these days. Why didn't the women notice that?

True enough, Sally hadn't been bringing women to meals. Mama's records you couldn't argue with. But the significance of the nonevents was another matter. And the best evidence would come from Sally himself. That's what Angelo had said to Gina, "If Mama wants to know, why doesn't she just ask him?"

"You tell me something," Gina said. "Would Salvatore tell Mama, or would he make a joke? Which?"

Which was fair enough. But hadn't Mama brought that state of affairs on herself by concerning herself so relentlessly with the state of Salvatore's affairs?

At the corner where Pierrepont became Manvers, a charity collector dressed as Father Christmas stopped Angelo and asked for a donation. "For the children," Santa said. "Ho-ho-ho."

Angelo fished through his wallet for a pound coin, thinking, Why me? Why does he stop me out of all these people on the pavement?

"Thank you and have a happy Christmas," Santa ho-hoed. Santa looked so young he could have been cutting school.

"Promise you'll ask Sally," Gina had said, "for Mama. Soon. All right?"

Angelo waited to cross at the pelican in front of Comet. Maybe there's something about me that makes people pick me out, he thought. The lights changed and the beep beep beep started. He crossed, wondering if he was being pitiful, fretting that the world picked on him. Boo-hoo, he thought. And then noted that boo-hoo wasn't all that different from ho-ho. All right, all right, all right, he would try to find a moment to ask Salvatore.

Pushing through the police station door, Angelo trotted up the two steps and turned to the window on the left. He asked the constable there to alert Charlie that he had a visitor.

The entrance area was not large, little more than a hallway with two doors leading off it. Somewhere inside the station a man shouted, "I ain't done nothing. I ain't! Why me?" and Angelo felt a moment of personal connection with him.

Then, shockingly, a door burst open. A small man emerged. Angelo saw denim, black hair, pink cheeks. Then hands from behind the man pulled him back. "I ain't done nothing!" the man cried. One of his hands grabbed at Angelo's arm. "Help me. They're trying to bloody fit me up, and I ain't—"

But the man's grip on Angelo was broken and he was dragged back through to the dark side of the door. Although it was not such a private place that Angelo missed out on a harsh voice growling, "Shut up, you little scum bucket."

"Are you all right, sir?" the constable on reception asked through the glass. "Not injured or nothing?"

"No. But what's that about?"

"Sorry, sir, I can't speak to you about that."

However Charlie was less inhibited, once the door to his computer room was closed. "Winston Foxwell," he said. "A little matter of a body being found under the compost heap in his back garden."

"Anyone he knew?" Angelo asked.

"I gather a dental ID just confirmed that it was his uncle."

"Charming."

"Especially considering that the skull had a whacking great hole in it."

"I take it he hasn't confessed yet."

"Other than making a run for it? Good as, wouldn't you think?"

"Meanwhile he's helping with inquiries, right?"

"Right."

"Funny that," Angelo said, "because I was hoping that you might help me with some inquiries."

"Are you coming?" Mama asked.

"What for?" the Old Man said. "Who needs me to come? Gabriella to fuss at me and tighten my tie?"

"You're never going to forgive her for that, are you? Or forget."

"She chokes me to death. That I should forget?" The Old Man loosened the tie with one hand and made as if to take it off. "Here, take my tie for her to tighten. Safer that way."

Mama watched as he held the knot above his nose, waiting for her to tell him not to take it off. "Just don't say I didn't invite you to come," she said at last.

As Mama put on a coat, the Old Man put his tie back to where he liked it, loose under his collar with the top button undone. For a client he would tighten, but not for Gabriella. Huh!

Then he saw that Mama was at the door. "Signing?" he said. "Are you signing anything?"

"Come and see, if you're so curious."

"I'm not entitled if you sign away my money?"

"Whose money?"

The Old Man was silent at this.

"It's in my account, so it's my money," Mama said. "Unless you plan to tell the tax man different from all these years all of a sudden."

"Who earned it? You?"

"Oh, I earned it," Mama said. "I earned it double, putting up with you so long."

"You don't like putting up, then don't," the Old Man said. "Put down, if that's what you like."

"Well, I'm leaving now. I'm meeting Gabriella and her Nina. We're going to make a list, if you must know. Things the landlord must do before we sign."

"What things?"

"Come along, if you're so curious."

"I just asked. You want I shouldn't show an interest?"

"Show an interest, if you want," Mama said. "And why not sign the lease too, and pay the rent."

The Old Man frowned so deeply his face felt furrowed even inside. What was the point of this, to become involved in a restaurant—a *restaurant*. At her age, and all of a sudden. He couldn't work it out. What was it for, her doing this, causing this argument? Most business you do to earn money, but that couldn't be her reason, because there was plenty, even plenty in her own name. So what for? The aggravation? The heartache? Because that's what a new business was. No, it made no sense at her age. If she was younger, young, like she was at the beginning, when she got off the boat, then there was time to start a business.

"Well, I'm going now," Mama said. "Last chance."

She was such a pretty girl at the beginning. She stepped off the gangplank and there was no disappointment. Not a bit. Pretty, and docile too. Biddable. In those days.

Celia Corman kept an eye on two young women who were browsing her racks as Angelo explained what he'd learned from Charlie at the police station. "There is an offense under common law called public nuisance," Angelo said. "It's called public but it can be committed in public or private places."

"And is that what the filthy creatures are committing, Mr. Lunghi? Public nuisance in a private place?"

"If they're committing anything."

"If?"

"If a police officer became convinced that what your Dirty Girls are doing here is part of a pattern of behavior, then chances are the officer would arrest them and let the court decide if they were breaking the law."

"Arrest them?" Celia Corman brightened. "You mean put them in jail?"

"Only briefly. They would be released on bail."

"Oh." Disappointment. Celia Corman called to one of the browsers, "We have that in pink too. Beautiful with your eyes." The browser nodded.

Angelo said, "At this point you need to decide exactly what it is that you want to happen from here."

"All I want is for them not to come back to my shop."

"So you aren't concerned with getting the money back that you've given them, or in having them prosecuted?"

"What I want is not to have to think about them. Couldn't you threaten them? Like with physical violence?"

"I'm not sure that would achieve your objective," Angelo said measuredly.

"But if you met them at the door when they come in today, maybe with a few friends. Big friends?"

"Suppose I did that, and suppose they went away. Would you feel confident that they wouldn't be back tomorrow?"

Celia Corman sighed.

"Wouldn't my big friends and I have to be here several days in a row? Which would both scare away at least as many customers as the Dirty Girls do now and cost you much more anyway."

"So what *do* you suggest, Mr. Lunghi?"

"Well, one plan would be to instruct me to follow them when they leave here."

Celia Corman frowned. "Why?"

"Chances are they are causing the same nuisance at other shops. If I can establish that, then it would greatly enhance the concept of 'pattern of behavior' and the chances of their being arrested and warned off by the police."

"And how much would my hiring you to follow them cost me?"

"Not nearly as much as Plan B."

"Which is?"

"Pay them a lump sum to stay away for good."

Mrs. Thompson, the school secretary, studied David's note and frowned. "Another visit to the dentist so soon?"

Mumbling because of the toilet tissue in his cheeks, David said, "Yuh, he boshed it up las tine."

Although David wasn't sure Mrs. Thompson understood what he'd said, she nodded, looked at her watch, and made a note of the time on David's letter of excuse.

Yes!

Mrs. Thompson asked, "Will you be back before the end of school?"

"I dunno zackly."

Mrs. Thompson held the letter up. David's heart pounded. "Will you be up to it after the treatment? Shall I ring your mother to ask if she wants you to come straight home?"

"No," David said clearly. "No need. No nee. See how I fee when he done."

"All right, then. Off you go."

"Fanks." David left the secretary's office as quickly as he could without his haste being unseemly.

Merde, he thought. That was close, too close. *Trop* . . . But he couldn't think of the French word for "close."

As the Old Man made his way down the stairs, he saw Rosetta on the lower flight coming up. "Hi, Papa," she called. "Are you having lunch with us today?"

"Lunch? Is it the time?" The Old Man looked at his watch. He hadn't thought about lunch.

"It is if you're hungry. And *I* am."

Rosetta stepped onto the landing that led to the kitchen door, and the Old Man watched his daughter cross one leg over the other. She spun. She put one heel out, then changed her mind and put the other out. She clapped her hands. What did all that have to do with hunger?

Rosetta said, "Gina and I are here for sure. Angelo might be coming. I don't know."

Gina's head popped out. "There's ham and *ciabatta,* if you want it, Papa."

"If I want, if I want." All of a sudden everyone says *if I want,* the Old Man thought. But who listens? Who listens what I want? Certainly not Mama, and her Gabriella's Nina. So why bother? Why go to this empty place they fill with lists? And maybe sign, who knows.

"Papa?"

"Lunch," the Old Man said, "why not? People must eat, lunch, dinner. That's why there are restaurants."

David froze where he was on the pavement as soon as he spotted his father talking with four women outside a shop. He hoped that he hadn't been seen, even though Angelo was looking his way.

David's pamphlet on surveillance said that a "visually vulnerable operative" should turn his (or her) back and move slowly out of the line of sight. So, adding the improvisation of a limp, David eased himself into the deep doorway of a shoe store. When at last he turned to look, he saw that his father was still talking intensely to the four women, obviously the Dirty Girls. What a relief.

From his position David couldn't tell how dirty the girls actually were, although their clothes were certainly shabby. What surprised him was how ill-matched they were. There was a very tall one and a very short one, a very fat one and a very thin one. One was redheaded, one was blond, there was a dark-haired brunette and a sandy brunette. From the way they had been talked about at dinner, he had expected them to be uniformly large, scary, and exotic. Now, all together listening to his father, the Dirty Girls seemed none of these things.

After a time Angelo reached into his pocket and gave something to the sandy brunette. And then he shook hands with her—actually shook her hand! The blonde stepped forward, as if to kiss him on the cheek. Angelo jerked back, but he laughed. The girls laughed too. Then they turned and began walking David's way.

David followed their progress from the corner of his eye, while trying to appear to be studying the women's shoes in the window before him. But then something surprising made him stand up and face the pavement as the Dirty Girls were about to walk past.

The sandy brunette noticed David's attention and tugged at the redhead's arm while pointing at him. The redhead waved. "Hi, Davy," she called.

5

*A*ngelo got to the office just in time for the pager client's two-fifteen appointment. Esta Dumphy wasn't there but Gina was, so Angelo reported the gist of what had happened about the Dirty Girls at Celia Corman's dress shop. "I threatened the police with one hand and gave them thirty pounds with the other—what they would 'earn' in a week."

"And you think they won't come back?" Gina said.

"Not to Corman, no."

"But you still don't know who they are?"

"The client didn't want to pay."

"And now we don't have a client."

"We have a *satisfied* client," Angelo said. "Papa would be proud."

"I wish I'd seen the Dirty Girls."

"Go to town, maybe you can. They must take their nuisance to other places as well. Think of all the money it made them from Corman."

"Five pounds a day?"

"Five places, ten places, it adds up."

43

"So you don't think they were genuinely needy?"

"No, a scam. They speak well and their eyes are bright," Angelo said as the doorbell rang. He went to the speaker. "Lunghi Detective Agency."

"Are you going to let me in or not?" Call Me Esta said. "I'm freezing my bollocks down here."

Angelo pushed the door release, but as he did so, he turned to Gina and said, "Is it cold? I was out and I didn't think it was particularly cold."

But this little mystery was resolved when Esta Dumphy bustled into the office in a short black skirt and the sheerest of black tights. "Phew," Call Me Esta said. "I'm perishing."

"Sit down," Gina said. "The chair by the radiator is the warmest."

"Thanks." Call Me Esta sat. When she had adjusted herself, she said, "So, have you found out who's been nine-nine-nining me? Because the bugger's been at it again. Once last night at what I must say was an awkward moment, and then already once again today."

"I had a talk with British Telecom this morning," Gina said. "And unfortunately if the pager 'message' is only a number, like a telephone number, the message is passed on automatically. Because no humans are involved, there are no records of the caller."

"So it would be better if he was saying, 'I'm going to kill you, Esta, so make your will'?" Esta Dumphy sighed deeply and grimaced. "I'm stuck with it? Is that what you're saying?"

"Oh, no," Gina said. "We may not be able to get the telephone numbers the nine-nine-niner is calling from, but there are other ways we can go."

Esta crossed her legs and rubbed the top leg's calf. "I'm still bloody freezing." She returned to Gina. "There are other ways we can go? So let's go. I need to feel I'm doing *something*."

Angelo said, "These nine-nine-nine pages are really upsetting you, aren't they?"

"They're bloody terrifying me, in more ways than you can understand."

Salvatore was sprawled across a couch in the basement café of the Windows Arts Center. "Corn chowder?" Heather asked.

"Yeah, great," Salvatore said. "And Earl Grey and a slab of that carrot cake, okay?"

"Whatever."

Salvatore straightened up to look into his shoulder bag, but Heather said, "I'm paying. My turn."

"Is it? Are you sure?"

"Trust me, honey."

"I wouldn't let you do what you do if I didn't, babe."

Heather smiled and went to the counter. Salvatore lingered on the memory of Heather's smile. It reminds me of something, he thought. I've got it. It's like old Mona's.

The Mona Lisa's smile was supposed to be big-deal enigmatic, but Salvatore didn't think of it that way. For him the smile's famous "enigma" was resolved the instant he covered half of Mona's face. The left half was smiling, the right half was frowning. Put them together and you have Mona's mystery. What was new now was realizing that Heather's facial expressions worked in something of the same way. Her face was always interesting to look at.

Salvatore wondered about painting Heather with the right/left thing in mind. Not mixing a smile and a frown—that had already been done, right? But how about mixing two other faces? A lustful face with . . . With what? A fearful face? Or, truer to her nature, a caring face.

Salvatore tried to visualize such a painting. But then he laughed. If essence-of-Heather was an issue, he'd have to have her dribbling from one side of the mouth. Such a detail was unlikely to enhance the commercial potential of the painting.

But bodies were expressive too. Body language. Suppose he composed a painting in which the two sides of her body read differently. Something more subtle than pull with one hand and push with the other. That might be interesting.

Heather slid onto a chair beside the couch. "What do mean, 'letting' me do what I do?" she said.

"I mean that what you do cures me of what ails me, babe," Salvatore said. "Hey, while you were gone, I got an idea for a picture. I want to do some drawings."

"Now?"

"You can eat first."

"Thanks."

"You don't have to be anywhere, do you?"

"Well, no. But—"

"Great." Salvatore opened his mouth, intending to explain the subject of his idea. But no sound came out.

"What's wrong?"

"See that boy who just came in?"

Heather looked.

"The one with the four scruffy girls?"

"Yeah. What about him?" Heather looked at the boy

again. "He's cute, but I hope if you paint him, you leave it at that." She made a face at Salvatore. It was not enigmatic.

"He's my nephew."

"Oh." Heather looked again, more interested. Then half her face frowned. "Shouldn't he be in school?"

"One option," Gina said, "is to try changing your pager number. If it worked, it would certainly be a lot cheaper than paying for us."

"But if he got my number in the first place, no reason to believe he won't get it again." Call Me Esta frowned. "It is likely to be a man, isn't it, what with it involving numbers and machines?"

Angelo said, "And because it is threatening an attractive woman."

"You are such a sweetie."

"But we won't be sure until we identify him, or her."

Gina said, "Do you have any idea who might want to threaten you?"

"No." Esta Dumphy uncrossed and recrossed her legs.

Angelo said, "Well, we'll need to go through some of your personal details so we can work out an efficient strategy."

"You're welcome to all the personal details you want. Has anybody ever told you what beautiful eyes you have? Of course they have, sorry. Sorry. Cold affects my brain."

Gina said, "Esta, who have you given your pager number to?"

"Just Jerry. He gave me the damn thing in the first place, and I only carry it so that he can page me."

Gina said, "And who is Jerry, please?"

"My lover," Call Me Esta said. "The last time I was here

you gave me a biscuit. Do you still have any? 'Cause I haven't had any lunch."

"Hello, David."

David turned toward the speaker of his name. "Uncle Sal. Oh."

"Shouldn't you be in school?"

The redheaded Dirty Girl said, "Go on, Davy, tell him why you're not in school."

"As you see, I'm not in school. In fact we're all not in school. As you see."

"I see," Salvatore said.

"And that's because, uh . . ."

"School is closed?"

"No, no," David said, not wishing to sign up for a story that could so easily be checked. "School is open. School is definitely open. But what we're doing here is, what we're doing is a study project."

"Studying coffee?" Salvatore said. "Or are you studying tea?"

"No, no. Neither. We're not here here doing the project. No, we're here here taking a break. For lunch. Which, after all, everybody needs to do when they're . . . when they're . . ."

"Doing a study project," Salvatore said.

"Exactly." David knew that his lame excuse had left him dead in the water.

But then a woman came up to Salvatore's side and slipped her arm around his waist. "Aren't you going to introduce me to your nephew and his friends?" The woman stretched out a hand. "I'm Heather."

"I . . . I'm David." They shook hands lightly.

One by one the four Dirty Girls shook hands with Heather and introduced themselves: Mandy, Ixy, Lindsey, Ruth.

"And you're working on some project, did I hear?" Heather asked.

"That's right," Ixy, the redhead, said.

"For our economics GCSE," Ruth, the blonde, said.

"It's about Christmas," Lindsey, the dark brunette, said.

"Obstacles to commerce," Mandy, the sandy brunette, said.

"Lack of money being the greatest obstacle," Ixy said. "To Christmas commerce, I mean."

"It's not a problem for those of us who celebrate the solstice," Heather said, "but I know what you mean." Then she squinted at David's forehead and touched it with her fingertips.

"What?" David reached for his forehead but touched Heather's hand.

"You have a bit of a rash. You ought to let someone see to that before it gets worse. In fact—"

"Come on, Heather," Salvatore said. "Let's leave the poor kid and his friends in peace. They've got their project to do."

Heather laughed as Salvatore spun her away.

And David was struck by how pretty she was, in a hippie kind of way. This one was rounder than a lot of them, but Uncle Sal's women were always wonderful.

Mama was not happy as she walked toward home. Nina, who was supposed to have the business brain in her marriage partnership, didn't seem to have brain of any description. Barely enough to tie a shoelace. Certainly not enough to plan a business. "If you think so, Mrs. Lunghi." "Is that really necessary, Mrs. Lunghi?" "I never thought of that, Mrs. Lunghi." Such an hour of didn't-thinks Mama couldn't remember.

Yet this, this macaroni head, this was what Gabriella praised to the sky and what Gabriella now expected her to commit money to do business with. It was all shocking. Mama was shocked.

It was not that a list of repairs hadn't been compiled for the prospective landlord. Any sensible woman could see what needed to be done. Where they intended to cook the food was a kitchen, after all. Where they intended to serve it was a dining room. What was so hard? But where do you plan to store your plates? "I never thought of that, Mrs. Lunghi." And what about a place to keep records and make telephone calls? "Is that really necessary, Mrs. Lunghi?" Surely you'll need to protect against cold drafts from the windows. "If you think so, Mrs. Lunghi."

What, Miss Nina Macaroni? Are all your diners going to be twelve years old and impervious to the cold? I don't think so.

And this was the business brain. Nigel was the cook. But Nigel wasn't there. Nigel left the business side to Nina. Nigel was still at college on his chef's course. Oh, dear. Mama was not happy.

What about this macaroni disaster could be reported to Gabriella? And what could *possibly* be said to Papa?

And what was to be done about Salvatore?

Softening the truth to Gabriella was a maybe. Saying nothing to Papa was conceivable.

But doing nothing about Salvatore was not an option. Something had to be done about Salvatore.

"Me having a lover isn't a problem for you, is it?" Call Me Esta asked. "Because with an attention-deficit husband like Erik, it's a necessity."

"Our problem," Angelo said, "is your nine-nine-nine pages, Mrs. Dumphy."

"Please, call me Esta."

"Esta."

Gina said, "The first thing we'll need from you is a list of the people who might have got the pager number somehow."

"How? I didn't give it to anyone."

"Well, you might have left it as part of an answering machine message . . ."

"Only Jerry has the number. And, by the way, he's the one who made me realize that I couldn't just ignore the pages, and he will be paying your bill. Can you invoice him direct?"

"Of course, if he agrees."

"He'll agree. But I suppose you'll want to speak with him."

"Yes," Gina said. "When might we do that?"

"Now?"

"Fine."

"Can I use your phone?"

Gina and Angelo sat together while Esta dialed a number.

"Hi. Me. I'm with the detectives even as we speak, and they want to come over."

While Esta listened to Jerry's response, Angelo said to Gina, "You go, or me?"

"Why not both?" Gina said. "Put the machine on. Rose will answer if she's here and not busy."

Meanwhile, Esta hung up and turned to the Lunghis. "He'll be waiting for us. Let's go."

"Where, exactly, Esta?" Angelo said as Gina took the phone.

"Bailbrook College."

"I don't know where that is."

"On the A4, east. Just past the roundabout there was so much fuss about."

"And what kind of college is it?" Angelo asked.

"It's a school for ATC. Air traffic control."

"Air traffic control?" Angelo said.

"Airplanes." Esta flapped her arms. *"Brum brum.* Air traffic control?"

"I didn't realize we had a school for that in Bath."

"Not just 'a' school. The top flight school in Europe." Esta paused for just a moment. *"Top flight?"* She looked at Angelo. "I'm not going to find that angels don't have a sense of humor, am I?"

When the Old Man came to the office, it was empty. Huh! Such a thing would not happen in his day. But after a moment he took the opportunity to settle himself behind Angelo's desk.

Although the office looked different now, it was still comfortable. As much as anything that was because Angelo had retained the Old Man's chair, the agency's very first chair. A crown he'd paid for that chair. Five shillings, old money. Nowadays tell them twenty-five pence and they would laugh. What can you buy for twenty-five pence now? Nothing that would last.

But then, then it wasn't the cheapest. How long ago was

that, this chair? The Old Man shuddered as he realized that he'd been sitting in the chair for more than forty years. Forty. Such a time. Such a time.

The telephone rang. The Old Man looked at it, a pale box with buttons and lights. One red one was blinking.

This phone was nothing like the old black phones. You knew where you were with a telephone then. Those days you dialed a number by dialing it. No buttons. No tip-tap-beep-beep like now.

The telephone stopped ringing before he had picked up the receiver. He picked up the receiver anyway. He heard Rosetta's voice. She was talking businesslike. "Rosetta?"

"I've got it, Papa."

"Thursday, dinner. You're cooking?"

"I always cook on Thursdays, Papa."

"Hello? Miss Lunghi?" a man's voice said. "Do we have a crossed line?"

Rosetta said, "Hang up now, Papa."

So the Old Man hung up. But he sat with his arms folded on his chest. Huh. Just "hang up"? No "please"?

Mama climbed the stairs to the office little more resolved about her problems than before. Even after a bite to eat and a slow walk, Nina Macaroni was no smarter and Salvatore was no closer to marriage.

It was not *that* foolish a plan, surely. To have financial interest in a café so that she could display Salvatore's paintings on the wall. The location was perfect, downtown near an art school, a center. Places where painting people went. And even painting people need to eat. Someone sees Salvatore's work. Someone buys it or commissions it or gives him a job teaching it, whatever happens to make painters feel successful. Confident. Ready to settle down.

Getting married . . . Well, married isn't what it was. But "paired." Salvatore needed a woman to look after, to look after him. To have family. Married wasn't what it was, but family was still family. Salvatore would make a good father. Mama knew he would. And being a father would be good for him too.

The idea of a baby, a small, fresh, new creature, made Mama pause on the stairs. Beautiful, wonderful things, babies. Who better to appreciate than a painter? A sensitive man.

Money in a café so she could have the walls might be an indirect way to help Salvatore find his destiny, but what else could she do that she hadn't already tried? A mother had to help.

Yet did a mother have to help when it also meant helping a Nina Macaroni? Mama shook her head and began to climb again.

What to do? What to tell Gabriella? What to tell Papa?

The only progress to answers Mama had made was that it would be good to talk with Gina. Hence the climb to the office instead of going up the parallel staircase that led directly to the flat. Gina would help. A good girl, Gina. The kind of girl Salvatore should have. Pity when Salvatore brought her home in the first place, all those years ago, that it didn't stick. Angelo would have missed out, but Angelo would have found another. He was never so much a problem that way. Never a problem like Salvatore.

At the landing Mama tapped on the office door and went

in. What she found was not Gina. Instead it was the Old Man. He was talking on the telephone.

"What are *you* doing here?" Mama said.

The Old Man put a hand over the phone and said, "Quiet, Old Woman. It's a murder."

6

$\mathcal{J}$erry Northam was middle-aged, good-looking, and immaculate in a three-piece suit. He was brief and clear in his summary of the air-traffic-control teaching and systems development that Bailbrook College offered. He held Esta's hand as he spoke.

Angelo said, "Thank you," when Northam finished.

"Can you stop these disgusting nine-nine-nine pages?" Northam asked.

"I'm sure we can if we identify the caller. How might the caller have got Esta's pager number?"

"I never gave the number to anyone." Northam looked at Esta. "That was the point. We each have a pager that is a unique conduit to the other."

"And your pager is like Esta's?"

"Identical."

"But you've never had pages from an unauthorized source?"

"Only Esta has ever paged me." Northam squeezed her hand. She smiled.

"And what happens?" Angelo said. "It rings?"

"Vibrates."

"They have a vibration mode," Esta said. "I feel Jerry's messages come in."

Northam patted her hand.

"But your husband doesn't know about the pager?"

"It's possible that he's seen it, but he hasn't said anything. Probably he hasn't noticed. Erik is very self-absorbed."

"And do you have a wife, Mr. Northam?"

"Yes," Northam said with a smile.

"Don't tease them," Esta said. "Not one he lives with, Mr. Lunghi."

"What I'm getting at," Angelo said, "is that although nobody was given the number, who knew there was a number to get? Let's think about that, Mr. Northam. If the mystery caller got the number through you, how could it have happened?"

"Well . . . I don't know."

"Do you pay for both pagers?"

"Yes."

"Is there someone who has access to your financial records and might see that you are paying for Esta's pager? Might the records even identify the account by her number?"

"They may well," Northam said, "but I still can't imagine who would see them. I don't use an accountant. I suppose theoretically my cleaner could find the file and winkle it out, but she hardly speaks English."

"Your cleaner?"

"I live in a flat here at the college. There are staff suites at the top of the accommodation building. Several of us live there and we share a cleaner. But I almost never meet the woman."

Angelo asked, "Do people in the college know about your relationship with Esta?"

"They might have seen us together," Northam said, "but there's nobody we socialize with as a couple."

"Are you there often?" Angelo asked Esta.

"Quite often," Esta said. Northam kissed her cheek. "When schedules allow. But we are both very busy."

Northam said, "I doubt anybody would look at Esta and say, 'That's Jerry's girlfriend.' The course students come mostly from abroad, and in any case, they live here only weeks at a time. The other college staff and administrative personnel are here for longer, of course, but we don't mix with them. Otherwise . . . Well, the miscellaneous staff—cleaners, maintenance, and people like the blip drivers—do come primarily from Bath, but, frankly, there really is very little chance of anyone showing up here who is from Esta's social circle, if you know what I mean."

"What is a blip driver?"

"Our students learn their skills on air-traffic practice screens. We call the pretend aircraft 'blips.' The people who make the blips behave like aircraft are 'blip drivers.' "

"Ah," Angelo said.

"The blip drivers sit in separate rooms. Most of them are youngsters. Blip driving is one of the few jobs that those endless hours kids nowadays spend on computer games prepare you for."

Rosetta gathered a stack of envelopes to be posted and left her room. But instead of going out, she stopped at the agency office. She hoped to catch Gina there. She wanted to tell her that there were signs that David had been hacking into agency computer files. He'd done it last night, for sure, in the Dirty Girls file. Rosetta wasn't sure whether Gina would mind, but she was sure that her sister-in-law would want to know.

But instead of finding Gina in the office, Rosetta found Mama, who was sitting with her elbows on Angelo's desk.

"Everybody goes out," Mama said. "So I guard the precious business. Could anything be more important?"

"Where is everybody?"

"Gina and Angelo I don't know. Your father, God help us, has gone to the police."

"Papa to the police? But why?"

"Murder he tells me." Mama threw her hands into the air. "Murder? Can you believe such a thing? All these years since the Norman Stiles we haven't had a murder, yet today he answers the phone and a murder comes in. So he goes out, and here I sit."

"The machine takes the calls," Rosetta said. "Or you could have told me. I was just down the hall."

"I was here. I had to sit somewhere. Why bother you? What you do is important." Mama dabbed at her forehead with a handkerchief and shrugged. "Is there something you want? Can I help?"

"I just came in for a quick word with Gina."

"So popular Gina is all of a sudden." Then Mama moved the handkerchief to her eyes and dabbed again.

Rosetta moved rapidly into the room and to Mama's side. She knelt on the floor and took her mother's hands. "Tell me what's wrong, Mama."

"Salvatore's what's wrong. I try and try and try so hard, but what thanks do I get?"

As they drove home, Gina suddenly said, "I've worked it out."

Angelo brightened, because he didn't feel he had a grasp on the pager mystery at all. "That's great. So, who's paging?"

"Oh, I don't mean that."

What else was there to mean?

"I know what's wrong with Jerry Northam."

"Wrong?" Angelo slowed to a stop in traffic at the lights controlling the turn to Cleveland Bridge.

"There was something not right about him."

"Not right? That's left." But Angelo wasn't dismissing Gina's feeling about the man. Gina's impression of people was right much more often than it was . . . left. "So what's wrong?"

"He was too attentive, too solicitous. He holds her hand. He kisses her cheek."

"That's wrong?" Angelo took Gina's hand. He leaned toward her cheek.

"Get off. I'm serious. This Northam is the kind who buys pagers because of schedules. But if he is so sure that he is not the source of Esta's number for the nine-nine-nine, he should be annoyed with her. And he ought to be fussing about the expense—how much money can he have? But instead he's all gooey-gooey. That's not right, unless he has secrets."

Angelo considered. Northam was certainly gooey-gooey. "What secrets? Something with the wife he jokes about?"

Gina considered. "Maybe that he has someone else."

"You get someone else from gooey-gooey?"

"He doesn't show off this beautiful Esta. Don't men like to show off their beautiful women?"

There was truth in that, Angelo thought. Lights changed and the traffic ahead began to move. He rolled down the car window and shouted to the people in the car next to his, "See this beautiful woman beside me? She's mine!"

"You, I understand," Mama told Rosetta. "From a little girl I always understood what you wanted. What flavor ice cream. What shoes. Always, I knew. Maybe sometimes you have bad luck, like with that married Walter."

"The newt," Rosetta said.

"And even now, when we don't hear much about this new one, this Christopher, still I understand my little girl. I know what you want. And I don't need to worry about you because you worry about yourself. But Salvatore," Mama said, "he brings me anguish. Doesn't he *want* a family? He must want a family. Don't you think your brother wants a family?"

"I'm sure Sally wants a family, Mama. I just don't think he's found the woman he wants to have family with."

"In that case," Mama said, tapping the wooden desktop with each word, "why has Salvatore stopped looking for her?"

"Has he?"

"All his life my Salvatore brings his women home. Even Gina he brought home from art college. But now, all of a sudden, after all these years, now it stops. Week after week, meal after meal, do we see Salvatore with a new woman? We do not! I go crazy. I mean this. I may do something foolish. Something that will cost money. Your father will hate me. It will be a divorce."

"Mama, if Sally isn't bringing women home, it doesn't necessarily mean he's given up on them altogether."

"What else can it mean?"

"Maybe . . ." Rosetta sought to choose her words carefully. "Maybe Sally does have a girlfriend, but maybe there is a reason why he doesn't want to bring her to the house."

"What reason?"

"Well, maybe there's something about her that would make him uncomfortable. Maybe something he thinks the family might not like." Rosetta strove to appear casual. "It could be that she was a black woman."

"Black he's brought before. Well, brown. But brown, yellow, spotted with pimples, even American, have we ever cared?"

"Or maybe she's older than he is."

"Older? You mean too old for children? Oh!" But after a moment Mama said, "We can send her to Italy. In Italy doctors do wonders. Did you read about the grandmother they made into a mother again?"

"Or maybe . . . maybe she . . . Maybe this woman has a job that Sally thinks you and the family would disapprove of."

"What job?"

"Oh, I don't know. But there are jobs you and Papa wouldn't, well, you might not want one of your children to be connected with."

Mama's eyes narrowed. "My Salvatore has a prostitute?"

"No, no."

"A massager? That's what they call them these days. I read about massagers."

"I don't mean that, Mama, but suppose she had a job like, oh, I don't know, pick one at random, suppose Sally was going out with an undertaker. How would you feel about that?"

David was careful to arrive at the house at the usual time. He was late if anything. He trotted up to the kitchen. "Hi," he called. "I'm home."

There was no response. A quick check showed that the flat was empty. David was surprised. Normally there was a bustle of activity as a mealtime approached, even though it wasn't a family night. If people were out, it could mean that interesting things were going on in the agency.

David's heart quickened. He dropped his schoolbag and went through to the office. But the only person he found there was his grandmother.

"You're home," Mama said.

"Where is everybody?"

"Out. So it's only me left to be concerned about family."

David saw his grandmother's face crinkle up. "What's wrong, Grandma?" He threw his arms around her.

"What's wrong? What's wrong? My Salvatore is dating an undertaker! That's what's wrong."

David's jaw dropped. The beautiful woman with Uncle Salvatore was an undertaker? Wow. Trust Uncle Sal. He could find them anywhere. "At least she's a pretty undertaker."

"You know her?" Mama said sharply. "You've seen this undertaker?"

An instant of hot panic served to remind David that when he had seen the woman he was supposed to have been in school. "I saw Uncle Sal with a woman, Grandma. After I got out of school." Which avoided a lie. "But I didn't know she was an undertaker."

"So, it's all true!"

7

*S*o she's an undertaker," the Old Man said. "So what?"

" 'So what?' " Mama said. "That's your only comment about your son's future?"

"So maybe we can all get cheap funerals."

Mama threw her hands up in disgust. At the kitchen table David sat watching his grandparents.

And at that moment Marie came in from school. Mama turned to her. "Cheap funerals. That's all he can say. What do you think of your grandfather now?"

"Did I miss something?" Marie said easily.

"Uncle Sal's dating an undertaker," David said.

"Male or female?" Marie was so pleased with the quickness of her response that she couldn't suppress a quick giggle, despite the fact that she and Cassie had agreed that it was naff to laugh at one's own jokes. But Marie cut herself off and said, "Are Mum and Dad in, creepface?"

"No," David said.

The Old Man said, "Undertakers she has on her mind. She doesn't even ask about my murder."

"Did you murder somebody, Grandpa?" Marie said.

"You could be murdered," Mama said. "It would be a reasonable thing for a father who neglects his children."

Marie went to the fridge for a bottle of diet cola.

Mama said, "And Salvatore will help with the burial, because his undertaker should get the business."

"When I say my murder," the Old Man said, addressing Marie, "I mean a murder case."

"The Norman Stiles?" Marie asked, pouring her cola.

"No," the Old Man said with evident pride. "A new murder. I was called out for it this afternoon."

"Really?" Marie glanced at David to see if this might be a joke-story she had missed the beginning of, but David's transparent face told her nothing of the kind. "You got a murder case today, Grandpa?"

"It's a murder, all right. I'm only just back from the police. And I tell you," the Old Man said, "I could really murder a cup of tea."

"Well don't look at me," Mama said. "I'm going upstairs. I have things to do. A man who cares nothing for his family can make his own tea." She rose from her chair.

"I'll make you a cup of tea, Grandpa," David said, jumping up. "You too, Grandma." But Mama left the kitchen without another word.

"You make tea, David," the Old Man said, "and I'll tell my grandchildren about the new murder."

"Great!" David said.

But Marie was in a quandary. If her mother and father stayed out longer, she might be able to leave the house for the evening without having to lie about where she was going. On the other hand, if she stayed to hear her grandfather's story, he might give her some money, and that would certainly come in handy because then she would not need to depend on George to buy her drinks. For sure Cassie wouldn't have any money, and a certain amount of independence was definitely desirable around a man like George. But how long would it be before her parents came back?

After a moment Marie sat at the table by her grandfather. If she hurried him along, maybe she could have it both ways. She said, "Someone asked you to solve a murder? Who?"

"It was a solicitor who rang. But it's all right. I knew this solicitor's father, who was also a solicitor. So I know this one will pay."

"And the solicitor killed someone, Granddad?" Marie said.

"Dummy," David said. "Solicitors call on behalf of clients. That's right, isn't it, Grandpa?"

"This solicitor behalfed a client, yes," the Old Man said.

"And did the client kill someone?" David said.

"The client denies, but in this client's garden they dig up a body. And the body has a hole in its head about this big." The Old Man held up his fist. "About the size of a *tea*cup."

"Oh, sorry." David turned back to the kettle, which was boiling.

As he did so, the door to the kitchen opened and Angelo walked in. "Teacup? What beautiful words. I could murder a cup of tea."

David laughed.

The Old Man said, "Huh!"

Marie jumped up from her chair, said, "Hi, Dad, hi, Mum," and left for her bedroom.

67

Holding the door for Gina, Angelo said, "What did I say?"

Salvatore gave Heather a kiss as she slept. For a while he watched her eyelids flicker as they followed events of a dream. Then he rolled away from her, eased himself off the foam mattress, and stood up.

Looking down at Heather, Salvatore liked what he saw. There was an innocence about her as she dreamed. She was not the prettiest woman he had ever known, but he could visualize her face in a variety of pictures, reflecting a variety of emotions, always with a dreamy innocence. Yes. This woman was special and he badly wanted to paint her.

Salvatore left the bedroom and went through to the kitchen of her flat. Tea would be good, he thought. He poured water from a bottle into a pan and turned on the gas. Yes, tea would be good, but some dinner would be even better.

He opened the small refrigerator. The top shelf was filled with bottles of clear liquids. Each was labeled with someone's name. But below the bottles there was food. Salvatore found three pears, a stick of broccoli, and a vegetable object he did not recognize. A carton of soy milk stood on the rack in the door.

He closed the fridge and looked in a cupboard. There he sorted through a collection of spices, a few tins of tomatoes, a sprouting head of garlic, and some paper bags—two containing carrots and potatoes and two containing more things he didn't recognize. But nothing he would call "real" food, nothing to make him salivate. He closed the cupboard door.

Oh, well, he already knew that cooking was not Heather's strong point. The taste of the food made in this flat was like Heather herself, often strange to him, and exotic.

But he was still hungry. The kettle boiled, and as he poured water onto a tea bag, Salvatore looked at his watch. There was just about time to go home for dinner. It was a Wednesday and there would be no big meal of the kind he fancied. But at least the food would be familiar and plentiful.

However, after a moment Salvatore realized that it would be better if he did not go home. Not when there was a risk that David would say, "Who was that woman I saw you with today?"

Even if Mama wasn't at dinner herself, it would get back to her. And sure as sauce was sauce, Mama would nag him relentlessly until Heather's existence was confirmed and a meeting was forced. That particular meeting was one Salvatore did not want to expose either Heather or Mama to. Not just now. Not yet.

So perhaps take-out food was the best option for the evening. Salvatore took out his wallet. Oh, dear. Which reminded him that he needed to ask Gina if there was some detective work that could be put his way.

What with a little teaching and a little illustrating he was about breaking even on rent and food, but now that he had paintings he wanted to do, a series of Heathers, he needed money for materials, paint, canvases.

From the bedroom Heather called out, "Salva? Are you there?"

Salvatore smiled as the call was repeated. Heather's sleepy voice was throaty and wonderful.

"I'm just going out for a few minutes," Salvatore said. "To get some eggs and cheese for an omelette."

"Great. I'm famished."

The first thing Mama did when she entered her flat was to put water on for a cup of tea. While she waited for the kettle to boil, she said aloud, "Yes, Gabby, of course I met your lovely Nina at the shop like we planned."

But Mama wasn't pleased with what she heard. Her voice didn't sound sweet enough. So she started again, "Oh, Gabby, your Nina is so pretty these days. I know we have other things to talk about, but every time I see her, she's prettier than the last time."

And stupider, Mama thought. But she liked the way this line of initiation sounded. It played to Gabriella's vanity about her children—Nina was pretty, Antonio the doctor was clever, and Sofia was graceful. Gabriella could talk like a record on the subject of her children.

All right, start with the children, Mama thought, and wait out the replay of the children's virtues. And then talk about the meeting and the lease. But how was she going to find a way to back out of the deal? That would be harder, much harder, because from the first time it was talked about, Gabriella taunted Mama with the prediction that the Old Man would never let her spend such money for herself, no matter how many years she worked in the agency, no matter how many hours she spent making it possible for him to do his detecting.

"I can do for myself," Mama had said, stung. "If I want." All of which meant that the easiest way to back out of the deal, blaming him, was blocked.

Mama considered for a moment how it would be if she spoke her true feelings to Gabriella. Could Gabby be told that her pretty Nina was a macaroni head? As Mama poured hot water to warm the teapot, she said aloud, "Gabby, is running a business really what Nina wants to do with her life?"

But Mama shook her head. Gabriella would know what was being said. Nina might be stupid, but Gabriella was not.

Or could Mama tell the truer truth? That she no longer wanted to invest in a café because Salvatore had a woman after all.

But that would be too galling. To admit that her sole reason for getting involved in the café was to provide walls for Salvatore to exhibit his paintings, to help him feel more self-steam about his career and to be more ready to meet a woman and settle down with her and become a grown-up with a family.

Everywhere you hear about self-steam these days, like on programs with audiences that should not be pooh-poohed just because they're Americans. It made sense. If Salvatore didn't feel his career had a proper head of self-steam, of course he wouldn't feel it was responsible to marry, or partner or pair or whatever it was that they did these days. And what should a mother do but try to help self-steam, especially if it was so bad he wasn't even seeing women at all.

Except, it turned out, he was seeing a woman. And suddenly Mama felt less need to throw good money after Nina Macaroni-head.

Mama emptied the teapot and made tea with boiling water. Could she possibly tell Gabriella that the deal was off because Salvatore had a woman after all?

Difficult. Gabriella would not like it at all—though she could perfectly well find the rest of the money for Nina herself if she truly wanted to. No, Gabriella would make Mama say everything about Salvatore out loud. And she would make Mama go over it. "I don't quite understand," Gabriella would say.

Mama wondered if she could explain her reasoning in a way that didn't let Gabriella treat it as a pathetic attempt to manipulate the beautiful and talented but irresponsible Salvatore into a settled relationship.

No, Mama would never speak aloud of such things. Not to Gabriella, at least. Not even if that made it hard to get out of the deal. Not even if it made it impossible.

Mama took down a cup and saucer. She poured a little milk into the cup and then sat down to wait for the tea to brew. As she sat, she put aside thoughts of the difficult conversation to come with Gabriella. Instead she returned to the subject of Salvatore. So he had a woman who was an undertaker. What kind of reason was that not to let the family get to know her?

When the telephone rang, Gina was closest.

"Hey, doll-face," Salvatore said, "when are you going to leave that ugly brother of mine and run away with me to New Zealand? I hear they have houses there that are actually built in trees. Doesn't that sound great?"

"Yeah," Gina said. "Are you paying for the tickets?"

"Ooo, what a painful and pertinent question, because, as it happens, I could use some paying work if you've got any for me."

"Probably we can help. Do you want to come over and talk about it?"

"Sure."

"We've got take-out Indian here. There's plenty, unless you're preoccupied with an undertaker."

"I'm very much alive, thanks, but I'm not free till later. But you can save me the leftovers."

"Okay. Oh, hang on just a moment."

"Sure."

Marie stood with her hand up, a sign that she had something she needed to say to her mother. "What?" Gina asked.

"I'm going over to Cassie's. I'll eat there."

Gina nodded permission.

"Cool banana!" Marie said, and she skipped out.

"Cool banana?" Gina said to Salvatore. "Have you heard 'cool banana'?"

"Only when I take off my trousers."

"I do hope it has some other meaning," Gina said, looking at the door Marie had just closed behind her. "What time do you want to come by?"

"Was that Uncle Sal?" David asked when his mother returned to the table.

Gina nodded. "He's coming over about eight-thirty. He wants some work," she said, addressing Angelo rather than David. "I said we probably have some for him."

"*Sag bhaji?*" Angelo said. It was a form of acquiescence.

David held out his plate and let his father spoon out some of the spicy spinach dish. He considered whether it would be safe for him to be around when Uncle Sal came. The three adults would be talking about the new cases, and that would be interesting. But the consequences of being caught having lied his way out of school were potentially nasty. Butchie Jamison's parents caught Butchie bunking off school and now the poor sod had to carry a card around and get each and every teacher to sign it at the beginning of each and every class. David would hate such a thing if it ever happened to him.

"Thanks, Dad," David said. "Could you pass the *Bombay aloo?*"

But supposing the *merde* did hit the *ventilateur*. Was it better if David was in his room where he could be summoned to explain himself? Or was it better to be out of the house, so they had some time to calm down?

All in all it was probably better to go out, he decided. Among other things, Uncle Sal was less likely to remember their meeting earlier in the day if David was not there to remind him of it.

"Mum," David said, "Lena's invited me to go to a juggling workshop tonight. Is it okay? I've done all my homework."

"Cool banana," Gina said.

Rosetta arrived at Bath Pavilion's Wednesday line-dance night a few minutes before seven-thirty, her usual time. Although the Pavilion was a gloomy venue, and the teachers did not teach particularly well, she always arrived early enough to take part in the instruction sessions. But even though Rosetta always stood near the front where she could see well and concentrated hard, inevitably she failed to grasp at least one step or one sequence in each dance.

However her failure to learn quickly no longer caused her

grief. The more confused the new dances left her, the more solicitous Christopher was when he arrived at about eight-thirty. And once Christopher explained a step or a sequence or a turn or a scoot, Rosetta got it. Immediately. Rosetta was his stone, the medium on which he could display his ability to communicate the intricate combination of foot movements, spins, and changes of weight that was line dancing.

Christopher was so good that Rosetta had already suggested that he start his own line-dance classes. "If you can teach me, you can teach anyone," she said. And although he pish-pished the comment and told her she was better than she thought, she believed that he was actually interested in the idea. So she intended to suggest it again, this time with an offer of practical help. There was no reason why she couldn't do the same kind of business and administrative things for Christopher that she already did for the detective agency.

But that was for later. For now Rosetta concentrated on Heidi, the teacher with long legs and a self-conscious giggle. Heidi was saying, "I don't know the proper name for this step, but Rodney calls it the ta-rah turn, because it's like you see when people go 'Ta-rah!' " Heidi demonstrated something impenetrable. Rodney, her favorite student, bowed. "See?" Heidi said. "Ta-rah!" Giggle, giggle.

As Marie turned into Upper Boro Walls on her way toward the Anchor, she suddenly realized that she had left her schoolbag in the hall at home.

She swore aloud and slapped herself on the thigh. It was potentially a bad mistake because if her mother noticed it—and she was good at noticing things—then she would know that Marie had not gone to Cassie's to do homework.

"I never said it was to do homework," Marie rehearsed, but it felt defensive. What were they doing instead? That would need some working out.

Suppose her mother found the schoolbag. Would that mean she'd call Cassie's house? Ooo, nasty. Not likely but certainly possible. Marie detoured to a phone box in Queens Trim. She called her friend, hoping she had not left yet.

"Oh good, you're still there," Marie said as Cassie answered.

"Yes," Cassie said. "Because I'm not coming out."

"What?"

"Mum absolutely refuses."

"But you have to. I'm out."

"I just can't, Marie. Sorry."

Marie stood silent, thinking. She could always turn around, not to show up. But then there would be no nut selling, no money. No money! "Well, I guess I'll just have to go anyway, if you're such a vegetable."

"You're really going to do it?"

"Sure," Marie said nonchalantly. "Where's the harm?"

"Oh, Marie!" Cassie's tone of voice made Marie even more pleased that she had declared she intended to go to a pub to meet a twenty-four-year-old who had been in jail and who she hardly knew.

"I need the money," Marie said. "And I also need you to cover for me if my mother calls. Tell her what we're doing is working out a dialogue scene for Drama."

"All right."

"It's a scene between a mother—that's you—and a deaf-mute child—that's me. Tell her I'm really into my part, and that's why I can't come to the phone."

As the Old Man walked up the stairs to his flat, he remembered how Mama had left the room when he began to tell of the new murder. Huh! he thought. Some interest she shows. Well, let her ask about the case. Let her beg. She had her chance, and instead she leaves. Aloud he said, "Huh!"

On the landing of the flat door he smelled food. Something with onion, and garlic. A tomato sauce. The smell made him sorry he had already eaten.

Which is not to say that he didn't like Indian food, though some was too spicy for him, and that's the kind they seemed to order most of downstairs. But this was, well, this was real food.

He opened the door and went inside.

"You're back," Mama said.

"I've left it with the children," the Old Man said. "Let them do the donkey work."

"What are you talking about?"

"The murder. But don't even ask."

"All right," Mama said. "You've eaten?"

"Yes, but not so much I wouldn't taste, if that's what you want."

David was surprised how calm he felt as he rang the doorbell. He was surprised again when Ixy answered the door herself. He had expected a parent or her younger brother Scott, his schoolmate. Which was not to say he was disappointed.

"Hi," David said. "How you doing?"

"Well, well, well. Look who's here."

"I hardly recognized you with a clean face and no spiderwebs in your hair."

"That's just business, isn't it," Ixy said. "What do you want?"

"Can I come in? It's cold out here." Ixy stepped aside and David entered. "I need a place to hang out for a while."

"Yeah?"

"When we met my uncle at the café, I was supposed to be at school."

"So?"

"Now he's coming over to the house tonight. My only chance is if he doesn't remember he saw me this afternoon, so I don't want him to see me tonight."

"Well, well, well. Aren't you becoming a bad little boy, David Lunghi."

"Not so much of the little, if you please. I'm just short for my height."

Ixy laughed. "Come to my room, then. Unless it's Scottie you want to hang out with."

"I'm not in the mood for Lego, thanks."

Ixy laughed again.

Marie arrived at the Hobgoblin two minutes after the appointed time. She paused inside the door, surprised how nervous she felt. It was a public place. What could happen?

But no other women were in the pub, except behind the bar. Not a single one. She felt out of place, very small, and very young.

Oh, well. In for a peanut, in for a cashew. She spotted an empty table by an alcove. She went to it and then asked the men at the next table if she could take one of their chairs.

"Sure, darlin'," one of the men, an old one with long, yellow-gray hair, said.

"Thanks," Marie said without smiling. She and Cassie had studied themselves in a mirror and agreed that they both looked much older when they didn't smile. She moved the chair.

As she settled herself, she tried not to make eye contact with anyone, but it was hard to keep from looking around the pub. Where was George? She was irritated that he was late. But maybe her watch was fast. She shouldn't draw conclusions without checking her facts; if there was one thing that growing up in a detective household taught you, it was that.

"Excuse me," she asked the old man with yellow hair. "Could you tell me the time?"

The man nodded. "Ten past eight, near enough, darlin'."

"Thanks," Marie said, genuinely irritated now because it was even later than she thought. She was about to get up and leave when a different man approached the table. He was tall and wore a spotted apron over pale jeans and a dirty T-shirt. He carried three empty glasses and was one of the staff.

"Excuse me," the man said.

"What for?"

The man looked down at her. He seemed tired and didn't smile. He looked old.

Marie frowned as she tried to work out what the year of her birth would be if she were nineteen years old. She and Cassie agreed it was better to say nineteen than eighteen when they were being asked if they were old enough to drink. Liars wouldn't say they were older than they had to be.

The man said, "I can take your order if you want a drink."

"Right. Sure. I'll have a rum and Coke. That's dark rum. Okay?"

The man nodded, but as he began to turn away, Marie said, "Wait. How much will that be?"

He told her the price and Marie opened her purse to see if she had enough money. She was short twenty-four pence in the coin pocket, but there was a good chance some loose change was at the bottom of her bag. She fished around, increasingly embarrassed that she wasn't finding any coins, just wadded up sweet papers and hairpins.

She was about to give up and order just the Coke, or the rum, when a male voice said, "I'll pay for that. And a pint and a shot for me. Got it?"

"Yeah," the barman said. "I've got it."

George pulled a chair from the neighboring table. Even sitting, he looked enormous in his black leather jacket and long white scarf. "Hi," he said.

Marie looked at her watch. "I don't have all night," she said. "The first question is, if I do what you want, how much are you going to pay me?"

8

When Salvatore arrived at a quarter to nine, Angelo was sitting in the living room with his feet up. "Hey," Angelo said.

"Hey."

"Care for a brew?"

"Sure. Shall I get them?"

"No," Angelo said, rocking forward. "Wench! Two beers here."

A moment later Gina arrived in the room with three opened bottles of beer.

"Thank you, wench," Angelo said as Gina sat down. To Salvatore he said, "You've got to know how. See me privately sometime."

Gina put up a finger and said, "Careful."

"Cool banana," Salvatore said. He took one of the beers. "So, shall we get down to business?"

"Sure," Gina said. "So, who's the undertaker?"

"What undertaker?" Salvatore said.

"Be like that," Gina said.

To Angelo, Salvatore said, "I think your wench may be a bit poorly, bruvva. She seems to have undertakers on the brain."

"I promised Mama I'd try," Gina said.

"She's looking for an undertaker?" Salvatore said. "Isn't she well?"

"Yeah, yeah, yeah," Angelo said. "Maybe it's time to get down to the business business."

"Suits me," Salvatore said.

Christopher said, "You've really worked this out, haven't you?"

"Except for where."

Christopher nodded.

Rosetta said, "Does that mean you'll consider it?"

Christopher looked at the sheet of figures in front of him. "A headset radio microphone?"

"You'll want your hands free. They're very expressive, if you don't mind my saying so."

"And a CD player with remote control?"

"So you can start and stop the music without having to go over to the machine. You could have a little holster for the remote. Which would fit in with dances like Smokin' Cowboy and . . ." Rosetta tried to think of another dance that called for miming the shooting of a gun.

"Derringer."

"Right," Rosetta said brightly. Christopher looked at the figures again. "So what do you think?"

Across the dance floor the Pavilion's deejay put on a new song. Christopher's eyes blinked. "I think I'll think about it."

He took Rosetta's hand. "Come on. This is good for Schottische."

Rosetta gripped his fingers and stood up. Schottische was a partner dance.

"What I don't get," David said, "is why you guys don't learn to juggle." He looked for three items to juggle. He gathered up three small, bean-filled teddy bears and juggled them. He did one trick, called the cathedral, but when he caught it, he stopped juggling, before he dropped a bear and spoiled the effect. He was having a good night.

"We're not all multitalented polyswats like you, little Davy."

"I'm not so little. In fact I've gained a lot of weight lately."

"You have?"

"Hey, I used to weigh seven pounds three ounces."

"Yes, all right, all right," Ixy said.

"Juggling's not hard."

"Lena what's-er-name's been teaching you, hasn't she?"

"She got me started, but now I've got a book."

"You think I could learn?"

"Sure. You want me to show you?"

"Not with my poor little bears, I don't," Ixy said.

"I've got balls, but not with me."

Ixy giggled. "That's a shame."

Sternly David waved a finger at her. "The first lesson is that jugglers don't make jokes about balls. Or knobs."

"What about knobs?" Ixy put a hand over her smile.

"The end of a juggling club is called a knob."

"Knob knob knob."

For a moment David maintained his sternness. Then he began to blush.

When Gina and Angelo finished going through what they knew about the 999 pager threats, Salvatore shook his head. "What kind of threat is a telephone number? I mean, what kind of *real* threat?"

"When a pager call comes through," Angelo said, "the recipient has to respond or risk missing something. So when the nine nine nine comes through, Mrs. Dumphy has to look at it."

"So?"

Gina said, "She says it upsets her."

"All right, it upsets her," Salvatore said. "I don't doubt that or question it. But I'm trying to think about it from the other end. Suppose you're the threatener. If you really want to *scare* her, would you choose to do it this way? Wouldn't nasty letters be better? Or messages scratched into her car's paintwork? Or—"

"Hide her makeup?" Gina said.

"Meow," Salvatore said.

"But I see what you're saying," Angelo said. "Nine nine nine is not an obvious choice."

"Sounds more like harassment," Salvatore said. "Or even a kid thing. Does it sound like a kid thing to you?"

"But suppose that the threatener doesn't want to get close to Mrs. Dumphy," Gina said.

"Letters you don't get close," Salvatore said.

"But there's a postmark," Angelo said. "And maybe handwriting is an issue. Not everyone has easy access to type-writers."

"It's computers these days," Salvatore said, "but you're right about that. I don't have access without coming here, or going to a place I have to pay. So what are you saying? That the threatener is afraid Mrs. Dumphy might recognize his handwriting?"

"Or her handwriting," Gina said.

"I thought your Dumphy said it was a him."

"She thinks it's a him, but we don't know for sure."

"But it's somebody she knows," Angelo said. "That makes sense."

"Knows well enough to be afraid his, or her, handwriting might be recognized kind of cuts down the list of suspects, doesn't it?" Salvatore said.

"Nine nine nine has other advantages over letters," Gina said. "Letters take time to get there. With a pager the threat is immediate. If the threatener knows Mrs. Dumphy's schedule, then he, or she, can interrupt her at specific places."

"Interesting," Angelo said. "I think maybe we missed out asking her for a list of the exact times these nine nine nines come through."

"You want me to get back to her?"

"What do you think?" Angelo asked Gina. "Do we turn Sally loose on Call Me Esta? Is it safe?"

"Why not safe?" Salvatore asked.

"I believe my husband is referring to his opinion that Mrs. Dumphy is unusually attractive."

"Stunning," Angelo said. "Nine out of ten catty owners surveyed agree."

"Well, why don't I give it a miss this time," Salvatore said. "As long as there's something else."

"Give it a miss?" Angelo said. "Give stunning a miss?"

"Yeah."

Gina and Angelo looked at each other.

"I always thought of you as a computer wonk," Ixy said.

"I am," David said. "But I'm other things too. I am a person of many wonks."

"So you won't mind if I call you a wonker?"

"Not if you do it carefully."

"So," Ixy said, "what wonk varieties do you lay claim to beside computers and juggling?"

"Well, I'm a detective wonk."

"What does that mean?"

"My family's business is a private detective agency."

"For real?" Ixy's face showed doubt.

"I'm third generation," David said. "You met my father."

"I did?"

"At the dress shop today."

"That was your father? I just thought he was some friend the owner brought in to strong-arm us out of the place."

"No. He was a private detective and she hired him to strong-arm you out of the place."

Ixy grinned. "He's a private eye? A real private eye? Hired to get rid of *us?* Wow! The others are going to love this."

"Why do you guys do that, by the way?"

"What?"

"Hang around stores being ugly."

"For the money, of course. People like you can busk, with juggling or singing or whatever. We can't do any of that. But we can act repulsive. It was Marie's idea."

"Marie's?"

"She didn't tell you about it? We take Drama together and we were talking about how expensive Christmas is and how hard it is to get part-time jobs."

"And Marie thought up being repulsive and being paid to go away?"

Ixy nodded vigorously. "But then, when we were working out what to wear and the makeup, she didn't like putting on the slime."

"What *is* that stuff?"

"Slime."

"I know, but what *is* it?"

"It's called 'slime.' It comes in a jar."

"But Marie loves money," David said. "She worships at its altar. She kisses its feet. I wouldn't have thought slapping some slime on her face would bother her if there was money at the end of it."

"I think she's got something else in mind," Ixy said. "She and Cassie."

"What?"

"Something with older men."

David leaned forward. "What with older men?"

"I don't know, little Davy. But then all men are older from your perspective, aren't they?"

Marie looked at her watch.

"C'mon," George said, "the night is young. Let me get you another drink."

"I thought we were here to talk business," Marie said.

"We are. We will. But that don't mean we can't have a friendly drink or two, does it? I'm having another. You suit yourself."

Marie frowned because she was uncertain what was acceptable and routine in a business negotiation.

George said, "In a minute I'll take you to me gaff and show you me goods." He winked and stood up.

Marie stiffened. Meeting George in public was one thing, but going to his "gaff" was another.

But then George sat down, buried his face in his hands, and said, "Oh, no."

A moment later a man and a woman arrived by the table. They were both even older than George. The man said, "Well, well, if it isn't little Georgie."

George said nothing.

The man said, "This here is Trish, Georgie. Aren't you going to introduce me to your friend?"

"Why should I?" George sat up and looked defiantly up at the couple.

"To be sociable." The man extended his hand to Marie. "I'm Alex."

Marie shook Alex's hand and then Trish's. "I'm Marie." She looked at her watch again.

"Going somewhere, Marie?" Alex said.

Marie was working out that she did not have much time before she should leave for home. "George and I were just coming to a business arrangement, so—"

"Working girl, are you?" Trish said.

"Well, I'm trying to get a little money together for Christmas, if that's what you mean."

With a grin Marie didn't like, Alex said, "I'm sorry to interrupt your bit of business, but George and I have a bit of unfinished business ourselves. Don't we, Georgie?"

"No," George said.

"Don't be like that." Alex took a handful of George's leather jacket.

"Gerroff," George said, pushing himself up out of his chair and trying to twist away from Alex's grasp. However Alex maintained his hold on the jacket, and after a moment the two men stood still, face-to-face.

"Best we conduct our business in a less public environment, don't you think, Georgie?" Alex said.

George didn't speak, but he allowed himself to be led toward the door.

"C'mon, you too, sweetie," Trish said to Marie.

"Sorry," Marie said, "I've got to go home."

Trish took a firm hold on Marie's arm. "Later."

"So tell me about this murder," Salvatore said.

"A solicitor called while we were out with the nine nine nine," Angelo said.

"Papa took the call," Gina said.

"Papa?"

Angelo said, "So Papa went down to the police station to meet the solicitor, and his client."

"Go, Papa!" Salvatore said with a smile. "Who's the client?"

"Winston Foxwell," Gina said. "Ten years ago, Winston's uncle disappeared suddenly."

"Meaning?"

"One day he was there, the next day he wasn't. No warning. No word to the family."

"He lived alone?"

"Yes, and he was ..." Gina consulted her notebook.

"Forty-seven years old, a builder and decorator, twice divorced and no children."

"Okay," Salvatore said. "I'm wit'choo."

"The house stood empty for several months, and then Winston moved into Uncle Foxwell's so that it wouldn't be left to decay."

"Nothing to do with it being a free place to live, I'm sure," Salvatore said. "Did Winston do this with the agreement of the family?"

"He says he did, but there isn't much family. He has a mother, who was married to Uncle Foxwell's brother. That's about it."

"Did they file a missing person's report?"

"Yes," Gina said, "but nothing came out of it."

"So meanwhile Winston moves into the house," Angelo said. "And he lives there alone just like Uncle Foxwell did, for a while. But as the years go on, Winston gets married and now there's a kid."

"Marriage, family, these things can happen," Salvatore said.

"Then," Angelo said, "a couple of years ago a builder's merchant whose land backs all the houses in Uncle's row—"

"Where are we talking, exactly?"

"High Terrace. Do you know it?" Gina said. "A little east of Lansdown Road about a third of the way up the hill."

"The 'terrace' is important," Angelo said. "Make a note."

Salvatore moved an index finger on the side of his head. "Mental note."

"The terrace is important," Angelo said, "because High Terrace is a row that doesn't have vehicular access except a wide lane at the front where you can load and unload but can't park."

"Then," Gina said, "about two years ago the builder's merchant went out of business and the land was sold. The purchaser applied to build some houses, but permission was only granted on condition that the purchaser put in a new road, which would give the High Terrace houses vehicular access at the back."

"Which would put thousands on the value of the High Terrace houses," Salvatore said. "We don't have a planning committee member who lives in one of the houses by any chance, do we?"

"Couldn't tell you about that," Angelo said, "but all the High Terrace residents think the new plan is great—except for Winston Foxwell."

"Who objects," Gina said. "He even hires himself a solicitor."

"Why?" Salvatore asked.

"Because," Gina said, "he said he felt a powerful obligation to keep Uncle's property exactly as he found it unless or until Uncle approved the change. Uncle loved his house, et cetera, et cetera."

"Builder and decorator," Salvatore said. "Yes, I can see that."

"But the planning committee overruled him, with the support of the other residents."

"And because Winston was the occupier, not the owner," Angelo said.

"Uncle Foxwell was never declared legally dead?" Salvatore said.

"No."

"And, at last, a few weeks ago the developer started developing," Gina said.

"And two days ago," Angelo said, "the developer developed the end of Uncle Foxwell's garden and the developer's bulldozer developed a buried body, a body with a thumping great hole in its head."

"Uncle Foxwell, I presume," Salvatore said.

"Confirmed by dental records," Gina said.

"And Winston?"

"Is endeavoring to assist the constabulary with its inquiries."

"And we," Angelo said, "are endeavoring to assist Winston and his solicitor with their inquiries."

"Hey, it doesn't have to be murder," Salvatore said. "It could just be that Uncle Foxwell fell accidentally and hit his head on his papering table and Winston couldn't afford a funeral, what with the fortune undertakers charge these days."

"That's not the police's working hypothesis," Angelo said.

Gina studied Salvatore's face curiously.

Mama waited to call Gabriella until the Old Man was dozing in front of the television. "Your Nina," she rehearsed, "she's so pretty, prettier every time I see her."

But when the phone was answered and Mama asked for Gabriella, she was told that her friend was out.

"Out? At this time of night?"

The Old Man started. "Out? Who's out?"

When Mama hung up the phone, the Old Man asked again, "Who's out?"

"You were until a couple of minutes ago. Out cold."

The Old Man rubbed his eyes and cheeks and shifted in his seat. "Someone went out. Or maybe I'm wrong."

Mama looked sternly at her husband as he squirmed in his chair to face her. But suddenly her mood softened. "No, you're not wrong," Mama said gently. "It's me."

"You're out?"

"I was making a bad joke. I'm in a bad mood. It was Gabriella who was out when I rang."

The Old Man continued to rub his face, but then he said, "So what from are you in a bad mood? What did I do that I don't remember?"

"It's not you." Mama lowered herself to the floor by his chair and took one of his hands. "It's this café with Nina. I'm not so sure now it's a good idea, but I can't think how to get out without being a fool."

"A fool? Huh!" The Old Man hunted for the television's remote control.

"I told Gabriella I would do a quarter of the lease for Nina. I don't want to let her down. But I don't want to throw away good money either."

The Old Man pushed mute on the remote. "So what's wrong with this Nina?"

"She has no business head. I never talked to her before without Gabriella there. The smart head was Gabriella's. I didn't realize."

"Maybe Gabriella will be by her side in the café too."

Mama considered this. "Maybe. Maybe."

"I have handcuffs you can borrow. Sneak up behind." The Old Man patted Mama's hand. "Now out of the blue I married a fool? So what does that make me? Huh!"

"What the solicitor wants," Gina said, "is anything that might give Winston an alibi. We have the date of Uncle Foxwell's last contact with a member of the family. The presumption is that the murder took place soon after that."

"And Winston didn't do it, right?" Salvatore said.

"Winston is as clean as a parrot's whistle," Angelo said. "He's as innocent as a premature babe."

"But the critical period is ten years ago," Salvatore said.

"Ten and a half years," Gina said. "Uncle Foxwell seems to have disappeared the night of Good Friday or on Easter Saturday."

Salvatore said, "So, which bit of this ancient history do you want me to concentrate on?"

"Uncle Foxwell," Angelo said. "Social life, activities. People he knew through his work. Neighbors. That stuff. Gina and I will take Winston. Because, bruvva, as it happens, I believe I've met the chappy."

Salvatore looked surprised.

"This morning when I went to see Charlie about another case, a man I now know to have been our client's client got away from the officers restraining him, grabbed my arm, and said, 'I ain't done nothing.' "

" 'I ain't done nothing'?" Salvatore said slowly. "What's he like?"

"Small, dark hair, pink cheeks, dressed in denim."

"And possessed of the gift of the gab. 'I ain't done nothing.' Oh, dear."

"I believed him completely and utterly," Angelo said. "Since we got hired."

"And we start right away?" Salvatore asked.

"Yes," Gina said.

"Wouldn't it be cheaper to wait, see what the police come up with, and then try to fill in the holes?"

"Cheaper, but slower," Angelo said. "Winston wants to be home for Christmas."

Gina said, "The solicitor doesn't want to depend on the police investigation because he thinks all they're going to do is try to nail Winston and to hell with any other line."

Salvatore said, "So do we know how Winston plans to pay for all this investigating?"

"We do."

"The lottery," Gina said. "He won just short of two hundred grand in the first draw of the year before last."

"And he still has it?" Salvatore said.

"His solicitor says he saved it," Gina said.

"Why? Did he know that he would have to pay for an expensive legal defense one day?"

As he walked home, David felt elated. He had not only put together a complete list of the names of the Dirty Girls, he had established that they were all members of Marie's drama class and could be located through the school. Moreover, he knew their hit list of shops and, generally, what their strategy was—act tough but run a mile if a shop owner played hard-ball.

And the discovery that the idea for ugly-busking was originally Marie's was pure bonus. He would not put it in his report on the case, but it would be juicy to hold in reserve, ready to be sprung on Marie at an appropriate juncture.

Yes, a good night's work. David visualized telling his mother and father about it, and he anticipated how proud they would be of his detecting precocity. *Très bien*, they would say. *Très très, très bien!*

It wasn't until he began to climb the stairs to the flat that David remembered why he had left the house in the first place. He looked at his watch. It was a few minutes past ten. Surely Uncle Sal had gone home, back to his beautiful undertaker. Now she was a bit of *très bien*, no question about it.

But suppose Sal was still here. David tried to work out whether he was more likely to avoid seeing his uncle if he entered the flat by the kitchen door or by the living room door.

Usually Sal hung out in the kitchen. That was because he liked to eat while he talked. So David opted for living room door. As he let himself into the flat, the first person he saw was his uncle.

"Ah, it's David," Gina said. "Had a good juggle?"

"What?" Oh, right, juggling. "Not very. I just couldn't get the new trick I was working on. Maybe it was because I didn't take my own balls."

Salvatore looked like he was about to say something, but then he didn't. David said, "Hi, Uncle Sal."

"Hi."

"Well, I'm going to my room now."

"See you in the morning, Son," Angelo said.

"Yeah, good night."

David wasn't at all confident that his uncle would keep silent about their earlier meeting. But at least now David could play the Dirty Girls card. He could say he bunked off school because he thought he knew who the Dirty Girls were, and look! He had come up with the goods. Maybe it would not be such a bad thing for Salvatore to rat him out after all.

David had almost reached his room when the telephone rang. There was a phone in the hall, so he answered it.

"Hi, Davy, it's me."

"Me? Who's me?"

"Ixy."

"Oh, hi." What could she want? Had he left something behind?

"You got home all right, then?"

"Yeah. Yeah, I did." Then, without being able to control himself, he said, "You stayed at home all right, then?"

Ixy laughed. Then he heard her take a breath. "Look, this may be crazy," she said, "but I really like your sense of humor. And I know you're young and all that, a baby really, but I had a really good time with you tonight and I was sorry when you left, and I didn't understand what it was about until a few minutes ago, but then I realized that I was really disappointed that you didn't kiss me."

David's jaw dropped. Kiss her? It had never crossed his mind for a minute. Well, not specifically. He'd never kissed anybody—well, not anybody he wasn't related to. And not that way, the way she was talking about.

"Davy?"

"I'm here."

Ixy laughed, but it sounded nervous this time. "You're so funny, and confident, and I thought, should I call him and tell him? And then I thought, why not, what the hell, the worst that can happen is that I am utterly rejected and humiliated and end up bitter and twisted and insane for the rest of my life."

David managed to clear his throat in a way that sounded a little bit like a laugh.

"So I wondered if you'd like to go out with me sometime. Or," she said with another nervous laugh, "stay in. I promise I wouldn't put any slime on."

She wanted to go out with him! Or stay in! To kiss!

"Am I crazy?" Ixy said. "Because I was pretty sure that you wanted to too, or else why would you have come over tonight? But then I thought maybe you didn't say anything or do anything because, well, I don't know, because of me being so much older and you being friends with Scottie and, well, I don't know."

David's mind felt blank. "Scottie who?"

Ixy laughed. More relaxed this time.

David remembered, Scottie was Ixy's brother, his classmate, the reason he knew where Ixy lived.

"So I was right. Good. Whew. What a relief. Because I was really worried. I've never asked a boy out before. Especially not a young one. Not that I think age is all that important. Or important at all. Not if you really like each other. Or at least might. Well, I don't really know. I've never gone out with a younger boy. Just older ones. But not much older. I wouldn't want you to think that." She paused. "Davy?"

David's face was so tingly he could hardly speak. She had taken his visit for a social call, not a business one. Well, why shouldn't she? He'd told her it was social. Sort of. What had he said? He couldn't remember. He couldn't remember anything.

"Davy? Or would you rather that I call you David?"

Barely being able to speak, David said, "Call me anything you like, but call me."

Ixy roared with laughter. But then she said, "I've got to get off the phone now. I'll see you at school tomorrow, all right? Before assembly, by the tuckshop?"

"All right." As David was trying to think of something snappy to add, Ixy hung up. He stood for a few moments, holding the phone.

Even when he hung it up, he stayed in the hall, stunned. Reviewing what had happened. He could hardly believe it.

And then the telephone rang.

David let it ring twice, trying furiously to think of something witty to say. At last he picked up the receiver and said the only thing that came into his mind, "Call me anything you like, but call me."

"Pardon?" a woman's voice said. "Do I have the Lunghi house?"

It wasn't Ixy! "Hello?" David said.

"Mr. Lunghi?"

"Yes."

"I'm WPC Dixon. I'm ringing from the Bath Police Station."

"You are?"

"We have an underage girl who says she is Marie Lunghi and that she lives in your house. Is that correct?"

"Uh, yeah."

"Well, Mr. Lunghi, Marie was discovered drinking in a public house. She was in the company of a known felon, and there is every reason to believe that she was offering him sexual services in return for money. In order to interview her we need you or her other parent or responsible person to come to the station. I do want to make it clear that we are not proposing to charge her at this time, but it is very likely that we will be cautioning her formally. We would also like to have a discussion about her future conduct."

"Marie?"

"Marie Lunghi. That's your daughter's name, isn't it?"

"Could you hang on just a second?" David put down the phone and sprinted to the living room. "Mum! Mum!"

9

Marie led her mother and father and brother up the stairs and into the kitchen. She felt humiliated and exposed and very, very tired. "I still don't know why you all had to come," she said once the door was closed. "It was so stupid and embarrassing."

"Don't talk to me about embarrassing, young lady," Gina said.

"Or about stupid," Angelo said.

"It was just a mix-up," Marie said. "A stupid *stupid,* embarrassing *embarrassing* mix-up. I may sue them for police brutality."

"Now who's stupid?" David said.

"Shut up, David," Angelo said.

Gina said, "Go to bed, Marie. If we talk about this now, we all might say some things that we'd regret."

"It didn't stop you back there," Marie said, "in front of that snooty WPC. God, I hate her kind."

"And what kind is that?" Angelo said. "The kind that doesn't go into pubs and break the law?"

"It's not against the law for me to go into a pub. And it's not even against the law for me to buy booze. What's against the law is for them to sell it to me."

"And what about prostituting yourself?"

"Maybe I *should* do it. At least that way I'd enough money to pay for a few drinks."

His voice rising, Angelo said, "Marie Lunghi . . ."

Gina put a hand on his arm. "Go to bed, Marie."

"Can I call Cassie first? She'll be worried."

"You'll call no one at one-thirty in the morning," Angelo said. "I doubt you'll ever call your Cassie again."

"Just try and stop me!"

"Go to bed," Gina said. "We'll talk tomorrow. Go on."

Marie left the kitchen without saying anything more, but as soon as she was in the hall, she could hear her parents begin to talk again. Their voices were unnaturally hushed. Obviously they were talking about her. But Marie was too tired to go back and defend herself. It had been a very long day.

First she went to the bathroom to wash her face. What she saw in the mirror shocked her. Streaks of mascara ran down her cheeks. They made her look like a zebra. She couldn't remember having cried. It was ugly and frightening.

In fact the whole thing had been one fright after another. And there was no payoff. It had all gone wrong. Maybe she should just have done the boring thing and asked her parents to provide ways to earn Christmas money. Anything but housework. She'd rather put gunk on her face than do housework.

Marie held her head over the sink. She turned on the taps

and adjusted the temperature of the water. But once a flannel covered her eyes, she began to shake. A wave of upset rolled through her whole body. She sank to her knees and leaned on the basin and buried her face in the soapy cotton and bawled. Tears came out, so fiercely and from somewhere so deep inside her that for a while she didn't know if she'd ever be able to stop.

After leaving the police station, Salvatore went to Heather's. He expected her to be asleep. He expected to be able to kneel on the floor and watch her breathe and dream. He expected to be able to stroke her cheek and slip onto the mattress beside her.

He did not expect her to be sitting at the plastic patio table she used in her kitchen. And he did not expect to find her there with a bent straw hanging from her mouth, its other end in a bottle.

"Oh, hi." Heather took the straw from her mouth. "You're back."

"Yeah."

"I thought you'd left me for a younger, thinner woman."

Heather packed up her straw, capped the bottle, and put it in the refrigerator as Salvatore said, "Yes and no."

"Tell, honey."

"There was an emergency with my niece."

Heather frowned. "Is she all right?"

"Physically, fine. But I daresay her pride will take some healing."

"Will I ever get to meet this family of yours?"

"One day. If you're good."

Heather wiped the tabletop. "Did you accomplish whatever it was that you wanted to accomplish with your brother?"

"They have some work they want me to do."

"And do you want to do it?"

"Yeah."

"That's all right then." Heather dropped onto the floor with her legs crossed tight as a paper clip.

"I don't know how you do that."

"Do what?" she said with a smile. She patted her legs, then her belly. She looked up at him. "How are you, honey?"

"Okay." Then, "My head hurts a little."

"I thought so. Come here." She patted the floor. "Heather can fix you."

"I know." Salvatore stretched himself out on the floor and put his head in her lap. "I've never met anyone like you for fixing me."

"I feel hurt," Angelo said. "I feel let down. Do you have enough of the duvet?" He switched off the light by the bed.

"At least *she* wasn't hurt," Gina said. "Give me a little more. If I start with more, then maybe by the end of the night I'll still have some left after you wrap yourself."

"Sorry, sorry, sorry." Angelo pushed the duvet toward Gina. "But can she really be so desperate for money?"

It was an old subject. Gina doubted there was any amount of money that Marie couldn't spend in a week. Well, maybe not Winston Foxwell's two hundred grand. "Marie and money."

Angelo sank into his pillow. "So what do we do about what happened? Ground her? What?"

Gina pondered. What exactly had Marie done? If one were to believe her version of events—which was not automatic—Marie was meeting a man who'd said she could earn money selling bags of Christmas nuts from a table in the street in Bristol. But the nuts turned out to be stolen, and while Marie was talking to the man, he'd been arrested for handling the nuts and other stolen goods. Yes, she'd let him buy her a drink. "Don't be stupid!" to the rest of it.

"So what happens next?" Angelo asked again.

"Sorry, I was thinking."

"Thinking what?"

"How dangerous can a man be who gets arrested for handling stolen nuts?"

"But she lied to us," Angelo said.

"She does that all the time."

"She does?"

"Not wickedly, but pushing limits, omitting bits, not telling whole truths."

"Like it was Marie who stole the nuts in the first place?"

"I'm sure she's not doing things like that."

"Yet . . ." But after a moment Angelo said, "I don't mean to doubt. She's good, however she acts."

"Maybe you should tell her that."

"I should?"

"Maybe that's it. She expects punishment, something to fight against. Maybe you could talk to her and just be hurt and unpunitive."

"It wouldn't scare her to have her father cry?"

"Something to think about," Gina said. "But really, it's best to forget about it till tomorrow."

"How do I forget about it?"

"I can take care of that." When Angelo hesitated, Gina laughed. "I can ask you to think about something else."

"What else?"

"Salvatore."

"What about Sally?"

"Why does he turn down the chance to work with beautiful Esta?"

"He's more interested in murder than nine nine nine?"

"Ah, but he turned her down before we talked about Uncle Foxwell."

"Oh, yeah. He did." Angelo considered.

"And don't say it's because he already has a woman because that never stopped him before."

"True." Angelo felt for a tissue and blew his nose.

"So let's look at the facts," Gina said. "He has a woman, but he doesn't bring her home. We offer him work with a beauty, but he turns her down."

"So what do you conclude, Holmes?"

"That this woman is special, different."

"How different? She has three heads?"

"Certainly different in Salvatore's head."

"Well, we knew already that this one's different," Angelo said. "This one's an undertaker."

Rosetta snuggled in Christopher's armpit. "I'm not being too pushy by doing some calculations, am I?"

"Not really," Christopher said. "I know you mean it well."

"I know how good you are teaching me, that's all."

"But there's a difference."

"What?"

"Between an avocation and a vocation."

"Say."

"I love to dance," Christopher said. "When I dance, I can forget everything else. All my troubles at work. My nana's illness."

"That's why I thought, well, if you like it so much . . ."

"But if dancing were to become my job, then maybe dancing wouldn't be dancing anymore. It might be like . . . like . . . Well, it might be like the difference between being lovers and being married."

Rosetta waited for a moment. It was the first time the word *married* had been used in their conversations. "Might it?"

"When you're lovers, being married seems like the same thing, only more so. But then, when you get married, it's different."

"I wouldn't know," Rosetta said.

"Well, you can take it from me."

"So, you . . . ?"

"I was married."

"Oh."

"But she died."

"I'm sorry."

"When I saw her there . . ." Christopher's voice fell away.

Rosetta turned over and held him until he responded. "We'll forget about you teaching."

"It's not that I'm not interested. I mean, maybe teaching it would add things that aren't available to me now. I mean, it's possible."

"It's not like you'd have to quit your job."

"No, I suppose it's not all-or-nothing, like marriage. I suppose it is possible to live together for a while, see if you like it."

Live together? Rosetta thought. He's talking about living together? Did I miss something here?

David couldn't sleep. After the excitement of Marie's *contretemps* with the police and subsequent return home, he'd felt ready to fall straight into bed. But no sooner had he slipped between the cool sheets than Ixy appeared in his mind, her ginger curls draped around her smile. And then David wasn't tired anymore.

Ixy. Could what he remembered possibly be true? That she'd called him and asked him out? Or in. That she'd wanted... It was hard to form the words even in his head, but she'd said it, aloud, she really had. She wanted to kiss him. Or rather, she'd wanted him to kiss her.

Was that different? Well, technically, yes. But it was no less dramatic, and exciting.

Mon Dieu!

Ixy had called him funny and confident. Or was it confident and funny? No matter. Either way she'd fixed that they should meet before school. And then? Would she drag him behind the audiovisual hut, unable to wait any longer to taste the special honey of his sweet lips?

An unlikely scenario, David knew, however much the idea made his skin tingle. Much more likely was that they would meet up after school. Or again at her house. "Or in," she'd said. It was virtually the promise of a snog.

Snogging in Ixy's bedroom... What a prospect. Wow. Way wow. Famine to feast.

Unless . . . Would all her interest evaporate after his first beginner's attempt? Oh, how humiliating that would be.

Lying in his bed, David kissed his hand on the triangle made by the knuckles of his thumb and index finger and the knob on his wrist. He kissed it several times, trying each time to isolate how it felt to the hand.

With his lips he could gather a bit of skin and pull on it. Is that what Ixy would want him to do? Or was that stupid, ignoring a basic difference between kissing a hand and kissing a mouth—where a hand has skin, a mouth divides into lips, and behind them teeth, and a tongue.

Ixy's tongue . . . Oh, dear.

David moved the site of his kissing practice to "lips" made by aligning his thumb against his index finger. He tried to stick his tongue through the gap, but it wouldn't go, not unless he opened a space on purpose. Is that the way it worked?

Inside his mouth he pushed his tongue out against his lips, but the results weren't conclusive because his teeth got in the way. What about the other person's teeth?

Using the fingernails of his free hand David simulated teeth behind his thumb-and-index-finger lips. He kissed the lips, opened a gap and pushed his tongue forward until he felt the fingernails. There was nothing nice about this hybrid practice mouth. Was that how he was going to feel about Ixy's real thing?

David leaned back and gave up on kissing practice. Instead he concentrated on the stars stuck on the ceiling above his bed. He could still make out the luminescent constellations even though the light had been out for a while.

Funny and confident. Confident and funny. The twin

compliments now hung around his neck like twin weights. When he'd gone to Ixy's, he thought he was doing detective work, so of course he was confident. But Ixy had believed him to be there as a man. Well, as a male—certainly not as an investigator. And as soon as they met in the morning, Ixy would be looking for him to make her laugh, confidently.

David sighed. He felt the heavy burden of the expectation.

10

In the morning the first thing Salvatore did was go to High Terrace. Number 7, Uncle Foxwell's, was a modest enough two-story, stone house. There was one large window at the front and two on the higher floor. The roof was highly arched, so it was possible that the loft had been converted into more accommodation.

The houses either side of Uncle Foxwell's were much the same, although Number 6's small front garden was overgrown. Across the lane, facing the High Terrace houses, were the back gardens of another terrace row positioned farther down the hill. Perhaps Low Terrace, Salvatore thought. But he could see why the residents of High Terrace would be eager to have vehicular access at the back. The lane at the front was just about wide enough to allow a small van to load and unload. But it led nowhere and could not possibly be used for parking.

Yet Winston the Client had opposed the plan for vehicular access at the back . . .

Salvatore walked to the end of the terrace. All of the

houses looked to be good, solid, middle-of-the-nonvehicular-road properties. Nobody seemed well enough off to have had the facade sandblasted clean of decades of pollution, but three of the houses sported painted fronts, and generally, there was an air of care rather than of neglect, bar the front garden at Number 6.

A path to the back ran down the side of the last house, Number 14. It wasn't clear whether this was a public right-of-way, but Salvatore treated it as such and found that the path connected to another that ran behind the terrace. It was an odd arrangement, because this path divided each house's back garden in two.

As he strolled behind High Terrace, Salvatore saw that most of the houses had flowers and patios in the bit of garden near the houses and vegetables and fruit in the more distant section. At the foot of the distant gardens there was a wall, and Salvatore could see signs of building activity on the other side. That would be where the new houses were going and where, presumably, the new access road would run.

When he got to the back of Uncle Foxwell's house, Salvatore saw that the wall for Numbers 1 through 6 had been bulldozed away. But now yellow police-incident tape circled what was left of the wall at the foot of Number 7's garden.

Salvatore did not know much about gardens and gardening, but what remained of Uncle Foxwell's looked "well-established," as television gardeners apparently called old planting. And "well-maintained." And it was in considerable contrast to the back garden of Number 6, which was as overgrown as its front.

Salvatore wondered if perhaps Number 6 was empty. Uncle Foxwell's house had been empty for a while before Winston the Client moved in. Maybe it had looked like Number 6 did now. Maybe all the neighbors had been glad when Winston the Client arrived.

Salvatore looked at the back of Uncle Foxwell's house. A roof window showed that the loft had indeed been made into a room. As well, an extension had enlarged the kitchen. Well, Uncle Foxwell had been a "builder and decorator." So he had built and decorated at his home.

A woman appeared in the kitchen window as Salvatore looked at the house. Small, dark, with glasses, she held a child at her shoulder. And, she did not look happy. She waved a fist at him and then opened her hand, waving it as if to shoo him away. This presumably was Mrs. Winston the Client. Salvatore nodded to her and moved along the path. He might well be coming back for a chat with her. But not now.

He had only gone a few steps when a soft, high voice hailed him. "Excuse me?"

He turned to the back door of Uncle Foxwell's, but the mother with glasses was not to be seen. "Excuse me?" the voice said again.

Then Salvatore saw a woman with white hair waving from the back of Number 6. He took a few steps toward her. "Yes, ma'am?"

"Can I help you with something, young man?" The woman was, perhaps, seventy with dark, bright, beautiful eyes and a face full of life.

"As a matter of fact you can."

"Would you like to come in for a cup of tea?"

Marie delayed her morning appearance for as long as she could without giving her parents an excuse to come to her room. Her plan was to behave as if it were just another day. But she did put on less makeup than usual. If they were going to say something, she didn't intend to make it easy for them.

When she got to the kitchen, only David and her mother were there. And toast and orange juice were out for her, as usual. That was good. Even better was that when she sat down, nobody spoke to her. Her mother was busy with something by the sink. Her father, who was doing something with rubbish on the landing outside the kitchen door, probably didn't even know she was there. Not even David spoke. Mind you, Little Brother looked like death. He had probably stayed up all night being a computer wonk. Wonk-wonk, Marie said, but only in her head.

"Good morning, Marie," Gina said. "Do you want a banana?"

"No thanks, Mum."

No harm there. Marie downed her juice and looked at her watch. "Come on, wonk. We'll miss the bus." She picked up her two pieces of toast and went to the coatrack.

When her coat was on, she was surprised that David was still sitting at the table. He looked preoccupied, maybe on another planet like wonks were. Wonk-wonk, she thought. "Mum, I think Wonk-wonk is ill. Maybe you better keep him home."

But suddenly David jumped up. "No way." He dashed to the coat rack.

"I want to see you in the office after school, Marie," Gina said. "No later than six."

"What about?"

"About last night."

"What about it?"

Her mother turned from what she was doing. "About how your life should change. I'd like to know what you think we should do."

"Do?"

"Do," Gina said forcefully.

"Go on," Angelo said as he came back into the kitchen. "Go to school."

"Venez, venez, merde-y tête," David called. He headed down the stairs.

Marie moved to follow her brother, but when she picked up her schoolbag, she saw that David had left his behind. She lifted it and showed it to her parents. "Look. I'm doing a good deed. I'm a new person." She spun out of the kitchen and down the stairs chanting, "Wonk wonk wonk wonk wonk . . ."

Angelo was first to the office. He put the kettle on and set out mugs. But then he went to the window. He looked out on to Walcot Street. He signed deeply.

It was the same old Walcot Street. The same street as when he was a boy. Across from the house there was the same steep hill up to the Paragon. The same scruffy garages at the bottom. But it felt like a whole different world now. Marie offering sex for money? Even if it was the complete misunderstanding she said it was, the fact the suggestion had been made at all marked today's world as altered from the world he'd known as a kid Marie's age.

So she wanted to rebel, to fledge, to free herself from the defining constraints of being a child in a family. Did she have to do it by going to pubs with felons?

When young Angelo had wanted to be a rebel, he'd

worked his way up into the Paragon back gardens. Getting to them unseen wasn't easy. More than once Paragon residents had complained to his parents. But still he went, because there were things to be seen in Paragon back gardens, and not just the condoms, cannabis plants, and topless women. In his day Angelo had also befriended caged bunnies, discovered a hoard of blank cassette tapes—stolen?—and sampled stocks of liquor lined up alphabetically in a shed.

But the idea of ever doing anything that might be seriously against the law, or outrageously dangerous . . . That kind of thing was for the stupid boys. Or the bad ones.

Marie wasn't stupid. Or a boy. But was she bad?

The world had altered. Maybe it should be neutered.

As Angelo continued to stare, the kettle boiled. He turned to it, aware that he had not warmed the teapot or got out the tea caddy. He sighed again and made the tea.

Gina came in with a handful of post. "Tell me," Angelo said, "is Marie bad, is that the problem?"

"She used to be bad, but now she's a new person."

"It bothers me."

"Me too. But of course she's not bad. Don't be stupid."

"So maybe she's stupid. So maybe she inherits stupid from her father."

"I could be convinced."

Angelo said nothing.

"Look, are you working today, because there's a lot to do. Or are you going on holiday?"

Angelo spread his hands. "I made tea."

"Can you pour tea? Or are you too stupid for that?" Gina sat on the office settee and began to open the mail.

· · ·

When the white-haired woman from Number 6 passed Salvatore a cup of tea, he said, "You're very kind. I can't think of anything I want more just now than a cuppa."

"You must be older than you look," the woman said.

The image of Heather lying asleep on the mattress, all curves, no straight lines, rose in Salvatore's mind.

The woman laughed. "Not so old then, eh?" She raised a finger and chalked herself a point.

"Do you read minds?"

"Hardly."

"You're still very generous to offer me tea."

"Are you certain? Or is it that when I see a stranger on the front path who comes around to the back, I wonder what he's up to? And it's easier to find out if he's sitting in my kitchen."

"So you're crafty, not kind?"

"The one need not exclude the other. Would you care for a biscuit?"

"Homemade?"

"Certainly not."

"And not a gardener either. Or am I being presumptuous? My name is Salvatore."

"Valerie." They shook hands, then Valerie went to the kitchen counter and returned with a jar of biscuits. She took two and dipped one in her tea. "Yes, you are being presumptuous. The state of my garden is not unconsidered. It is merely untended. It's a mini–nature reserve."

"Oh, yes?"

"It was my daughter's idea. I admit I was reluctant at first, but in this day and at my age one mustn't be inflexible. Do you agree?"

Salvatore thought again of Heather, just for a moment. "I agree."

"You wish there were a little more flexibility at your home, don't you?"

"How do you *do* that?"

"Your face tells me where your attention is."

"If I book a session, will you sort out all my problems?"

"Don't be silly," Valerie said.

"Phew."

"It would take at least two sessions." As Salvatore was thinking, Really? she said, "I'm not a counselor. I'm not anything like that. I'm a widow with a curiosity about people and a daughter who lives south of town with a man who is jealous of her talent. All right? So who are you?"

Rosetta did not stay long in Christopher's flat after he left for work in the morning. Usually when she slept over, she spent at least an hour cleaning the place up for him. He never asked her to do it, so it was okay from a PC point of view. And Rosetta didn't really mind. They hadn't been "together" long but she was happy, for the first time in ages. This morning, however, Rosetta wanted to go home and sh
e didn't want to leave it until the afternoon.

When she got to Walcot Street, she used the office stairs. Gina and Angelo were on the settee. "Hi, y'all," Rosetta said. "Yee-hah!"

"There's tea in the pot," Angelo said. "Pull up a hitching rail."

"Thanks." Rosetta poured a cup of tea and dropped into one of the easy chairs.

"What brings you to the office so early, Sis?"

"I wondered if Mama said anything about Salvatore last night."

Gina said, "We didn't see her or Papa. But Sally came around. He's working on the murder."

"So you don't know if Mama's decided to sign the lease on the shop?"

Gina and Angelo looked at each other. "What lease?" Gina said.

"What shop?" Angelo said.

"She didn't tell you? I was sure she told you. I mean, I know she intended to."

"You'd better bring us up to speed, Rose," Gina said.

"Well, yesterday Mama told me she was having to decide whether to sign a five-year lease on a shop. But she couldn't decide whether it was the right thing to do."

"Why does Mama want a shop?" Angelo asked.

"I'm not quite sure, but it's something to do with Salvatore's not having a girlfriend."

"But he does have a girlfriend."

"He does? Well, Mama didn't think so when I talked to her yesterday afternoon. And he hasn't brought one to dinner for months."

"You don't bring yours to dinner either."

"But that's different."

"It is?"

"Number one, Christopher works a lot of unsocial hours, and number two, Mama isn't worried about me the way she is about Salvatore. She told me yesterday. She knows I want a family. It's Sally she's worried doesn't."

"Sally doesn't want a family?" Angelo said.

"Mama's afraid he doesn't. And, somehow, that's why she

119

wants a shop. I think she intends to run it as an art gallery or something like that."

"What on earth does Mama know about running an art gallery?"

"Nothing. And I think maybe that's what worries her. But there's something else, something about Gabriella's daughter, Nina. I think Nina is going to sell coffee and cakes or something."

"So it would be a gallery café?" Gina said.

"Something like that. I should have paid better attention, or taken notes. But as soon as she told me about it, I began to wonder if maybe the shop had a spare room, like maybe a room upstairs, because if it did, maybe Christopher could run some line-dance classes there."

Gina and Angelo looked at each other. Angelo said, "Clump, clump, clump, while people drink coffee and look at pictures?"

"I don't know," Rosetta said. "Like maybe in the evenings, when it was closed."

"Except," Angelo said, "he works evenings, your Christopher, doesn't he? Or is that just evenings we have family meals?"

"It's not like that. Don't be mean. And it was just an idea."

"Does Christopher want to teach dancing?" Gina asked.

"I sounded him out about it last night," Rosetta said with a smile. "And he said he'll think about it. So I want to be ready with a concrete suggestion if he decides he wants to do it. Which is why I wanted to talk to Mama about her shop, unless you already knew she'd decided not to lease it. In which case I'll look elsewhere. Okay? Angelo, why are you looking at me funny?"

"I never realized my little sister was such a package of convoluted planning, that's all."

"Don't mind him, Rose," Gina said. "Mama didn't talk to us about her plans."

"So I'll go up and see her in a while."

"Good."

Angelo said, "Are you still cooking tonight?"

"Sure. Do you know if Sally's coming?"

Gina and Angelo looked at each other. Angelo said, "He hasn't said anything."

11

$\mathcal{A}$s Lucy Davenant struck Angelo as very young to be the solicitor in charge of a murder case. Not that he would bet much on his ability to fix people's ages these days. Was she maybe early thirties, in her bright blue suit that set off sandy curls and pink cheeks? Certainly she was young-looking to be conducting a life-and-death. Perhaps the firm's name, Davenant & Davenant, offered an explanation. "Which one are you?" he asked as he sat down. "Davenant or Davenant?"

Lucy Davenant, it turned out, had a braying laugh that rocked the shade of the lamp on her desk. Angelo was quite taken aback. But as her laugh finished, she said, "As a matter of technical exactitude, Mr. Lunghi, I'm neither. Davenant was my grampy and Davenant is Dad. Grampy's gone now, but Daddy's still here part-time. I am a partner, but it didn't seem worth the bother to make it Davenant & Davenant & Davenant. And, my little brother Zeke is about to qualify too." Lucy Davenant rattled the shade again.

Angelo said, "Was it your father who used to work with mine?"

"Yes. Once Grampy retired, whenever we needed an investigator, we turned to Mr. Lunghi. Including one previous murder case."

"Norman Stiles."

"Well remembered! Because, as I understand it, that case was many years ago."

"Yes, it was." If Lucy Davenant wanted to think he was a memory genius, fine, even if the truth was that Norman Stiles was the only murder case the Lunghi Detective Agency had ever been hired to work on. Scratch a finger and produce a single drop of blood and try to stop Papa from telling the whole story over again.

"Your father's quite a character, isn't he?" Lucy Davenant said. "We had a good laugh together yesterday. And, I must say, he speaks very highly of the way you run the agency these days. I hope my father thinks half as well of me. Well, maybe three-quarters. Hay-hay, hay-hay, har-har."

Angelo waited for the lampshade to settle before he said, "Papa reported the basics to us. But if I understand them correctly, it may be quite a job to help your client."

"Mr. Foxwell assures me he is entirely innocent."

"The problem is that all the critical events seem to have taken place many years ago. Am I correct that the body was buried all that time where it was discovered?"

"There has been no suggestion to the contrary." Lucy Davenant looked at a few papers in the file on her desk. "About ten and a half years."

Angelo spread his hands to indicate that her response

proved his point. "Do the police have enough to charge Mr. Foxwell?"

"No, in my opinion. All they have is that he benefited from the murder."

"And that he was against the access road."

Lucy Davenant rubbed her hands together for a moment before saying, "Mr. Foxwell's objection to the access road was more active than that. He hired this firm to present his objection."

"And spent a lot of money?"

"A fair amount. Well into four figures."

"Of his lottery winnings?"

"So I understand."

"Isn't the intensity of his objection to the access puzzling?"

"Perhaps. But not criminal."

Gina contacted Esta Dumphy by paging her. In the half hour before Esta rang back, Gina dealt with the morning post. Half an hour after that, they were sitting face-to-face by the window of one of the French-style cafés in Shires Yard. "Thank you for meeting me at short notice," Gina said, "but Angelo and I agreed that we need to ask you some questions before we can have a reasonable chance to track down your caller."

Esta looked at her watch.

"Are you in a hurry?"

"No, but I may be getting a nine nine nine soon."

"You know when to expect the calls?"

"Not exactly. But weekdays, if the calls come, they come at about five past the hour."

"And do they only come on weekdays?"

"No, no. Any day. Or in the evenings. But in the evenings and on weekends they seem to come at any time."

"Angelo and I had a meeting about your case last night with Angelo's brother, who also works in the agency."

"There's something so sweet about that," Esta said. "Big family, all working together in harmony . . . It makes me teary."

Mama's distress about Salvatore and Marie's encounter with the police popped in and out of Gina's mind. "Our family's not all that harmonious."

"Even so."

"Esta, we wondered first whether we might not have been asking the wrong questions yesterday when we met with Jerry."

"Meaning?"

"We concentrated on who could have your pager number. We didn't ask who, exactly, knows you have the pager."

Esta said nothing.

"You said you and Jerry got the pagers solely to contact each other. And that your husband hasn't mentioned noticing. But you wear it on your belt. Have other people mentioned it or made clear that they've noticed it?"

Esta seemed about to speak when a waiter came to the table with a *cafetière*, two cups, and a fruit pastry for Gina. "Can I get you lovely ladies anything else?"

Esta said, *"J'ai changé d'avis. Je prendrai un pain au chocolat, à condition qu'il soit chaud mais que vous vous ne le soyez pas."*

"Uh, was that a *pain au chocolat?*"

"Yeah." The waiter left. Esta stiffened.

"What?" Gina asked.

"The pager just went off."

Esta took the device from her belt. She looked at it and then passed it to Gina. On a tiny screen Gina read, *999*.

"Now turn it upside down," Esta said.

Gina made the number into *666*.

"That's how I feel about it." Esta closed her eyes and put the knuckles of one hand to her mouth. She sighed. She shook her head slowly.

When Esta opened her eyes and looked again across the table, Gina said, "You know who's responsible, don't you?"

"Yes."

"I didn't do nothing, Mr. Lunghi. I didn't do *nothing*. That's why all this is a crock and shouldn't ought to be allowed." Clearly, an extra day's incarceration since Winston Foxwell grabbed Angelo's arm had not softened his sense of the injustice of his situation.

Lucy Davenant said, "Mr. Lunghi accepts that completely, Winston. Don't you, Mr. Lunghi?"

"Of course."

"Because I didn't do nothing, I really didn't."

"I've engaged Mr. Lunghi to help prove that," Lucy Davenant said. "But he needs to ask you some questions about your uncle and the time he disappeared. We only have a few minutes before Sergeant Mortimer wants to interview you again."

"Mortimer don't know his ass from his lughole," Winston Foxwell said. "Nor his lug from his—"

"Please, Winston, listen to Mr. Lunghi and do your best to answer his questions."

"I really didn't do nothing, Mr. . . . What was your name again?" But then Winston Foxwell fixed his eyes on Angelo. "What you want to know?"

"Susan has always been such a dark child," Esta said. "Not just in appearance, although she's that as well. Her hair's nearly black and her skin has always been sallow."

"How old is she?" Gina asked.

"Seventeen."

"And . . . Is she in school?"

"She's brilliant at school. It's her A-level year and her teachers will die of shame if she doesn't get four A's."

"So is she going to university?"

"She'd be an Oxbridge cert if she could do maths."

"Maths? What subject does she want to read?"

"Biology."

"She's a scientist?"

"Yes, but a nonmathematical one who is brilliant at art too. She won a special award for a project based on some nature drawings. That's the event I was buying a dress for when I met your husband. She's one of a group of North Somerset secondary-school children who are being given gongs for outstanding achievement."

"Congratulations. And are you close to Susan?"

"No. Nobody is."

"Her father . . . ?"

"Doesn't know her. It's not Erik. I don't even know where Randall is now. Probably pushing up daisies in Santiago. Or Sutton Coldfield."

"And why do you think Susan is responsible for the nine-nine-nine pages?"

"The way she looks at me."

· · ·

When Angelo's few minutes with Winston Foxwell were done, he made his way from the interview rooms near the police cells to Charlie's office. "Short time no see," Charlie said.

"I was already in the building, but if I'm taking liberties, please tell me," Angelo said.

"I can always say no. At least you didn't have them call me out last night. This is about Marie, isn't it? Do you want a coffee?"

"Yes to a coffee. And, yes, Marie is one of the reasons I'm here."

They made their way to the coffee machine. Charlie said, "What in the world is Marie hanging around with scum like George Skillman for? My treat. You take white without sugar, right?"

"Today I need sugar."

Charlie deposited coins and pushed buttons. Angelo took a deep breath. "What kind of scum would that be exactly?"

"The Skillmans are one of the families in town that everybody here knows. There are maybe ten families like them. And if all the members were locked away, then half the lesser crimes in the city wouldn't happen."

"Half? Really?"

"Doesn't seem possible, does it? But it's true. Or, at least, CID says it's true." Charlie handed Angelo a cup and they walked down the corridor. When they turned into his office, Charlie closed the door behind them. "Let's have a look." He clicked his mouse and brought up a file that included a mug shot. "Pretty, huh?"

Angelo looked at the screen. The face staring out from it was so obviously trouble that he could not comprehend how his little Marie could even consider dealings with it.

"This Skillman is George Herbert. He's twenty-two. His arrest record . . ." Charlie clicked again and the computer replaced the picture with a long list. "Yes, it already fills more than one screen, though the first actual conviction wasn't until he was fourteen."

"What kind of arrests?" Angelo asked quietly.

"Most petty enough—like what they're doing him for now. Handling stolen nuts, if I remember correctly. GBF was ranting about it when I came in."

"GBF?"

"Oh. A CID officer we call Girl's Best Friend."

"Because he isn't, I presume."

"Bit of a rough one, GBF." Charlie clicked his mouse. "Yes, stolen nuts and chocolates. But George Skillman's been up for violence too." More clicks. "Participant in a fight outside a pub three years ago. And demanding money with menaces later the same year. Well, had to celebrate turning nineteen somehow, didn't he?"

Angelo shook his head again.

"So what's Marie's problem?"

"She doesn't think she has one. Maybe that's her problem." Angelo sipped from his coffee. "However, that's not the only thing I came in to see you about."

"Your Dirty Girls?"

"Not them either."

"What?"

"Winston Foxwell."

"Oooo."

"Or, to be more precise, the missing person's report that was filed when his uncle disappeared."

When Salvatore did not find either Gina or Angelo in the office, he went to the kitchen. It wasn't quite lunchtime, but with tonight being a family dinner night eating lunch early made sense.

But instead of Gina or Angelo, Salvatore found Rosetta. His little sister was slicing bread. "Yo, Rosie."

Rosetta turned as he spoke. As she did, Salvatore was struck by the expectant innocence of her expression. It transported him instantly back to when she was a child, days when he was at art college and she was finishing primary school. His little sister had always been open, trusting, and optimistic.

Rosetta said, "Hi. You looking for Gina and Angelo?"

Instead of answering, Salvatore went to his sister and enveloped her in his arms and hugged her.

"Okay, okay," Rosetta said, "I'll cut you a sandwich. Sliced pork and mustard all right?"

"I just remembered how nice it is to see you."

"Really?"

"Really."

"But you'll still have the sandwich, right?"

Salvatore laughed. It was agreement. He sat at the table and turned a page of the newspaper there.

"Are you eating here tonight?" Rosetta asked.

"Who's cooking?"

"I am. *Strozza preti* with a mussel sauce."

The image of the family table filled with steaming food made Salvatore salivate. "Make enough for seconds. I'll leave my collar at home."

"Just where is home these days, Sally?"

"What do you mean?"

"It's almost impossible to catch you in."

"There's a machine."

"So you're there and not answering?"

"What cross-examination is this?" Salvatore said. "I thought Winston Foxwell was the accused."

"Mama's worried about you."

"Mama's always 'worried' about me."

"This time is different."

"What different? She's worried that I might get married after all? Bummer! And just when I've found a nice Italian girl who wants to have fifty children."

Rosetta stared at her brother. "That's a joke, right?"

Salvatore laughed.

"It's driving Mama crazy."

"What's driving her crazy?"

"You've stopped bringing women home."

Salvatore frowned. It wasn't the complaint he'd expected.

"Mama says it's been more than three months since you brought a 'model.' "

"She counts?"

"Of course she counts. She worries about where all the women in your life have gone."

"So she wants me to bring a woman? It will make her sane and everybody else will get off my back?"

"Yes. For a little while, anyway."

"Why didn't somebody say, if it's so important? So tonight I'll bring a woman."

"You will? Tonight?"

"If she's free. But I expect she will be."

12

As the Old Man began to descend the stairs, he whistled. There was a tune in his head though he couldn't remember its name. Or many of the lyrics. Except for *amore,* but then most tunes had *amore,* didn't they? It was as if there was nothing else to sing about. Huh! But he continued to whistle until he heard two voices from the kitchen as he neared the landing. Why not stop in, say hello, be friendly?

He whistled the tune through once more. As he did so, the kitchen door opened and Salvatore emerged. "You sound cheerful."

"Why shouldn't I be cheerful? What's surprising? I can't be cheerful?"

Rosetta emerged. "Hi, Papa. Coming in? I'm making coffee."

"Sure. I'm cheerful. Why not? Be friendly, right? You too, Salvatore?"

"I was just on my way out, Papa. There's work to do."

"Painting work, or real work?"

As Salvatore took a breath, Rosetta said, "Sally's helping on the Foxwell murder case."

"The murder?" the Old Man said. "A murder can be tricky. You have to be careful with your facts. Like Norman Stiles."

"I'm trying to make sure to do everything the way my father taught me," Salvatore said.

"Huh!" With his arm the Old Man gestured for Salvatore to let him pass into the kitchen. "So go if you're going. It's work."

"See you later," Salvatore said as he trotted down the stairs. "See you tonight at dinner."

"He comes to dinner?" the Old Man asked Rosetta.

"Yes."

"He'll bring someone?"

"He says he'll try."

"Your mother's going crazy."

"I know, Papa. I know."

They both heard the door slam at the foot of the stairs.

The Old Man remembered now, Rosetta was in the flat in the morning. He said, "She felt better, talking with you."

"I'm glad."

"So I want to thank you."

"Thank me, Papa?" Rosetta was obviously surprised.

"I shouldn't thank my daughter when she does something good?"

"It . . . it just doesn't happen often. I think . . . Well, usually I think you don't notice what I do, or don't think much of it, because it's not detective work out on the street."

"But you handle the money. Without you, they're all out on the street." The Old Man nodded down the stairs.

"Especially *him*. Even though he seems to like it poor."

"Oh, Papa."

The Old Man saw that tears were forming in Rosetta's eyes. "What? What?"

Angelo studied Charlie's printout of the missing person's report filed on Uncle Foxwell, aka Phillip, by his sister-in-law.

Zena Foxwell rang her brother-in-law at seven-fifteen on Good Friday evening to invite him for Easter dinner. She said he sounded normal and accepted the invitation. But he didn't show up for the meal. After dinner Zena sent Winston around to the house, but he came back to say the house was empty. After a week without hearing from Phillip, the family went to the police.

Two days later, PC Duncan South called on the immediate neighbors. When those inquiries produced no sightings of Phillip Foxwell subsequent to the Good Friday phone call, South arranged to meet Zena and Winston the next day to break into the house through the front door. This they did, although soon after they realized that the back door was unlocked.

In his brief report South said nothing in the house suggested that Phillip Foxwell had left for a trip. His wardrobe was full of clothes. His passport and suitcases were in the bedroom. There was no sign of a struggle, nor did anything indicate he had been unexpectedly interrupted. South noted, for example, that no dirty dishes were out, although Zena and Winston said that the missing man was in any case very orderly. They also agreed that things looked as if Phillip Foxwell had just walked out of his house on impulse and never come back. At the end of the visit, South said, Zena Foxwell took a set of keys away and said she would see that the house was made secure.

At the end of his report South expressed his opinion that the disappearance was "suspicious." He also noted that nothing in his examination of the house looked like stolen goods.

There was no note of CID, or anyone else, having done any further work on the case. And nothing suggested that any related information had been obtained from other sources.

"Stolen goods?" Angelo said. "Why should he say nothing was stolen goods?"

"Phillip Foxwell was a fence," Charlie said. "Your lawyer didn't mention that?"

"I was told he was a builder and decorator."

"And that Winston didn't do it, I bet. There's no fountain of truth quite like a lawyer."

Angelo said, "So the dead man had a criminal record?"

"Oh, yes. Not the quantity of arrests your Marie's George Skillman can boast, but he was streaks ahead on quality."

"Please don't call him *Marie's* George Skillman."

"I'll try to remember." Charlie gazed at his computer screen, tapped some keys, and then clicked his mouse. "Your Phillip Foxwell certainly dealt in bigger booty than stolen nuts. Let's see, he was questioned about stolen kitchen appliances, cigarettes—lots of cigarettes—liquor, and even about money laundering. Maybe he used a stolen washer-dryer. He was arrested a few times too, but in the ten years before his disappearance the only conviction was an assault. Rather like your Marie's—"

Angelo raised a finger. "Don't even say it."

• • •

When Mama returned to the house, she found the Old Man at the kitchen table with Rosetta. He was eating ice cream. By the bowl was a plate with crusts of bread. "You've forgotten we have dinner tonight?" Mama said. "You'll spoil your appetite."

"Hi, Mama," Rosetta said.

"You go out, I get offered lunch," the Old Man said. "I'm supposed to say no?"

"Eat what you like," Mama said. "Just don't complain when you can't finish what's on your plate tonight."

"Tonight's tonight and now is now." The Old Man looked at Rosetta. "Now my daughter feeds me and I'm grateful." He took another spoonful of ice cream. "See?"

Mama shrugged. "Me, I'm grateful to our daughter too."

"How did Gabriella take it?" Rosetta asked.

"She will talk to her Nina. She'll ring me."

"How did you put this plan to this friend who wants to spend your money?" the Old Man said. "You said, 'Gabby, your Nina is a macaroni-head, so maybe my wonderful Rosetta should handle the business so it shouldn't go bust?' "

Mama said nothing for a moment. Then she laughed.

"Huh." The Old Man laughed. "Huh!"

"I said, 'Gabriella,' I said, 'Nina is so charming and pretty she should concentrate all her time with the customers.' "

"Macaroni-head." With a long exhalation the Old Man whistled.

"I said, 'Gabby, this morning I talked to my brilliant Rosetta and asked if she would help with the numbers and the business side. I hope that's all right.' "

"And did you ask about the rooms upstairs, Mama?" Rosetta said.

"I said the café should start downstairs, daytimes, if it starts. Build to a full restaurant if it works. Meanwhile use the rooms upstairs for other things."

"Like hiring them out in the evenings to help the cash flow?"

"Gabby said, 'What other things?' and I said, 'That's a business decision.' Ask my Rose for suggestions."

With a big grin on her face Rosetta clapped her hands. Then she tapped each heel twice.

Gina did not know who might be at home when she got back to Walcot Street. She found Rosetta, Mama, and the Old Man sitting together in the kitchen. They were chuckling, smiling, and obviously in a good mood. "Have I missed a party?"

"We're just talking about macaroni," Rosetta said.

"It has a hole in the middle," the Old Man said. The others laughed.

Gina was about to ask another question but the telephone rang. "That may be Angelo," she said, and answered it.

But the voice was a woman's. "Mrs. Lunghi?"

"Yes."

"I'm calling from school about David."

"What about David?"

"Well, I'm afraid that when he arrived at school this morning, he was sick, on the pavement outside the front door. One of his teachers saw him and brought him to the nursing station. We wanted to send him home, and his sister offered to escort him, but he's such a reliable boy, such a good scholar, that he simply wouldn't hear of it. So we kept him here all morning."

"Is he all right?"

"To be frank, Mrs. Lunghi, he looks terrible. Pale, drawn . . . Has he been sleeping all right?"

"As far as I know."

"Because he looks as if he's been awake all night. I wondered if he's been worrying about something. Or whether perhaps he had a reaction to something at the dentist's."

"The dentist's?"

Dina heard motion at the other end of the line and then David said, "It's nothing, Mum, honest. I'm fine."

"But if you were sick—"

"It was hardly anything. Only a little on my sweater, and hardly any volume overall. And I don't want to come home, Mum. I mean, not early. I'll be back at the usual time—well, a little later than usual probably. But there's nothing to worry about. They're just fussing here. . . . Yes, I mean you, Mrs. Thompson. I'll be back at the usual time, Mum. Or later. See you then."

The phone was hung up at the school end.

"What's happened to David?" Mama asked.

"I'm not at all sure," Gina said.

The address for Zena Foxwell on the police missing person's report was in Oolite Road. Angelo's map showed it in an area of the city called Odd Down, possibly because it was up, on one of the hills that surround the center of Bath.

At first Angelo thought he would check the phone book to see if Zena Foxwell—how many could there be?—had moved in the ten years since she reported her brother-in-law missing. But then he decided not to bother. He was interested in the neighborhood Winston Foxwell had lived in at the time of the crime. As well, there might be neighbors who remembered the Foxwells even if Mrs. Foxwell was now elsewhere.

But when Angelo rang the bell, the woman who answered it said, "I'm Zena Foxwell. Who are you?"

She was five feet tall, about fifty, and her graying hair in tight curls made a halo behind her face. Angelo gave his name and explained that he was working for the solicitor who was representing Winston.

"My poor boy," Zena Foxwell said. "If it's not the one thing, it's another."

"Has Winston had a lot of troubles?"

"Wasn't the DHSS up here, asking their questions, just last month? They don't have his current address on their computer. Can you imagine that? He's only been where he is now for years. It's not technically his own place, but he gets mail there. He's had a baby there. But that's not enough time for the bloody DHSS to get him straight on their computer, is it? What do we pay our taxes for? Eh? Eh?"

"Why did the Social Services want to know his address?"

"Nothing to do with him, of course. Wouldn't hurt a fly, my poor Winston, or claim a bean. But the nasty money-grubbing, moany-groany piece of work he's married to, that's a different story. Look, you going to stand out there on the step all day? 'Cause the cold wind's giving me the grippe, or worse. It's winter, in case you hadn't noticed. What did you say your name was again?"

Angelo followed Mrs. Foxwell to a sitting room and sat in an armchair as she left the room to make tea. As he dropped onto the cushions, he felt a crowd of faces staring at him. The room was filled with photographs. They peered out of their frames from every level surface except the floor.

After a moment, Angelo pulled himself out of the chair to take a look. He hoped that he would get an idea of what the members of the Foxwell clan looked like, perhaps even the late Phillip Foxwell. But he was disappointed. All the photographs were of television actors.

Angelo was studying "Vera Duckworth" from *Coronation Street* when Zena Foxwell returned carrying tea things on a tray. "I met her myself, you know. In the flesh. That picture's signed to me. Look, go on."

Angelo picked up the frame. On a postcard-size photograph *Love to Zena, X* was written in black ball point. The signature, *Elizabeth Dawn, "Vera,"* was written in blue.

"She carries the cards already signed, y'see, and when she meets you, she writes the personal message on. That's how she does it."

"Ah." Angelo looked around the room. He guessed there must be a hundred framed pictures. "And you've met all of these?"

"Oh, yes. I wouldn't have them in the house else. I know there's lots who write a letter and get a picture back in the post, but that's not for me. If I haven't looked them in the eye, I won't have them in my lounge." She swept a hand around. "This way they're like family, y'know. If you've got only the one child, and a daughter-in-law like the devil, then you've got to make up the deficit somehow."

Angelo was about to ask about the daughter-in-law, but another question pushed it aside. "How do you meet them, these people? Do you travel around the country?"

"No, no. What I do is I work as an extra, mostly for TV, but I've done three films as well. I've been on ever so many programs. Maybe you've seen me." She fluffed her hair with a hand. "Take that one, Vera. *Coronation Street* came to Weston-super-Mare. I was Second Woman on the Beach. I wasn't credited, because I didn't speak. But I have spoken. I had two lines in *Casualty* just last year. Caring Mother I was. Two lines. 'I been waiting for two hours. What's the ideal?' And, 'It was that nurse what-'is-name, he took my Bernard, in there.' "

"Great," Angelo said.

"I have that look, you see. Motherly, caring. I get a lot of them. Been doing it for years. Hard work, mind, especially the waiting around. If you can't wait, you won't last. There's some that can't cut it, but it suits me."

"And can you make a living as an extra?"

"A living? Oh, good heavens no. But then I do have my Frankie's pension, God rest his soul. The extra work provides the extras, that's what I say. It provides the treats. The presents for little Phil—that's my grandson. No matter what *she's* like, I wouldn't take it out on little Phil. Some might, but that's not me." Mrs. Foxwell spread her hands. "What can I say?"

In the middle of the afternoon Salvatore stopped at Heather's flat. He found her in the bedroom, stretched out facedown on her mattress. Two men sat on the floor near her. Salvatore smelled incense.

"Hey babe," he said from the doorway.

In a muffled voice Heather said something that was probably "Hi."

"I bought a few canvases, and some paints. I'm going to leave them in the living room. Okay?"

"Okay."

Salvatore unloaded his purchases. Then he came back. One of the men he recognized, Running Bear, aka Running Bore. "What you doing? Can I watch?"

"Nasrullah is showing me what happens with magnetic healing."

Nasrullah was presumably the man he did not know. "Something wrong?"

She lifted her head. "We may work together."

"Please!" Nasrullah said with a frown. "You'll spoil it."

Running Bore said, "Prevention is always better than intervention."

Salvatore lifted one hand and said, "How." He heard Heather chuckle into the pillow. "Instead of retention it's my intention to go out, babe. I've got an interview to try to do."

"Okay," Heather said.

"And it's a family dinner night, don't forget."

"About your brother-in-law, Phillip," Angelo said.

"Totally different from my Frankie," Zena Foxwell said. "Fish and fowl, even if they was twins."

"I didn't know they were twins."

"Hour and twenty-three minutes apart. My Frankie took so much time they almost give up on him coming out. Always the slow one."

"So they weren't identical twins."

"Definitely not identical. Phillip was Mr. Tidy-boots. My Frankie was a slob. My Frankie loved his football. Phillip'd rather go dancing."

"Did they get along?"

"You can say they did, because they loved each other like, well, like brothers. But on the other hand they didn't spend much time together. Well, they wouldn't, 'cause of their different interests and that. But after Frankie left us, Phillip looked after me and Winston. Made sure we was okay for money till the pension clicked in and got the paperwork for this flat sorted. But I was already well into my extra work by then, so there wasn't all that much for him to do."

"How did your husband die, Mrs. Foxwell, if you don't mind my asking?"

"Hit and run on a zebra crossing. Some bugger on a Harley mowed him down." She sighed. "Frankie lingered for the best part of four months after, but then he kicked it."

After a moment Angelo said, "My understanding from the police is that Phillip Foxwell was a fence."

"They never convicted him of it though, did they? He was forever being pulled in and hassled, but they never found a single stolen good on his premises. Leastways nothing that I ever heard about. And he didn't never live flash or nothing. I think it's like that DHSS that's after Winston's address, only the reverse."

"How do you mean?"

"I figure the coppers got our Phillip onto their computer off some dipstick giving his name for no good reason, so then, whenever they was looking to hassle somebody, they pulled Phillip, but not because he ever actually did anything."

"He was convicted of an assault."

"A totally different thing. That was family, that was. He was defending Frankie at a pub. Nothing to do with fencing. My own Winston got done for the similar, when some bloke said something cockeyed about Sheila—that's her he's married to now. He was just with the wrong woman in the wrong place at the wrong time."

"Outside a pub at closing time?"

"Exactly. *And* it was on a night that I was on the TV. I told him, I said, 'You should of been here with me, watching my acting, instead of going out with that slag.' But he's never been lucky, my Winston."

"Mrs. Foxwell?" Salvatore asked the pale woman who came to the door of Number 7, High Terrace.

"Who wants to know?"

"My name is Salvatore Lunghi. I work for the detective agency hired by Winston Foxwell's solicitor to assist in his defense."

"Hired?"

"That's right. May I come in and talk with you about your husband and about his uncle?"

"I never met the uncle."

"But this was his house, wasn't it?"

"Used to be."

"And a nice place too, I understand." When Sheila Foxwell didn't respond, Salvatore added, "I was told it's been well modernized and decorated."

"I think you'd better go."

"Excuse me?"

"My Winston doesn't like me talking to men."

Without being able to help himself Salvatore surveyed the woman before him. She was slight and square and her complexion made him think of a corpse. "I can certainly understand why, Mrs. Foxwell, but I am working to try to help him."

"So you say. But he still wouldn't like it." She shook her head. "No, he wouldn't." Behind her a baby cried.

"Well, suppose a female member of our agency were to come here. Would you talk to her?"

"Female? You mean a woman?"

Salvatore sighed. "Yes." Not even a transsexual, he thought.

"I should think that ought to be all right. If it's necessary."

"I think we'll do it that way then. Bye now." Salvatore turned and left Mrs. Foxwell to close her door on his back.

13

*H*e's bringing a woman to dinner, Mum," Marie said.

"So I understand." Gina paused over the vegetable chopping board. "But how did you know?"

It was not the response Marie had expected. "How did *I* know? How did *you* know, that's the question."

"Rosetta told me." Gina returned to slicing peppers.

But this information served to complicate the mystery for Marie rather than resolve it. "But Auntie Rose can't know. I'm the only one who knows. Apart from *ooh-la-la* himself, of course."

"Who is *ooh-la-la?*" Gina said without looking up. "One of the Teletubbies?"

The notion of her brother as an infants' television star with a coat hanger projecting from his head pleased Marie greatly. "Good one, Ma."

"I don't understand what you're on about, Marie. But we have other things to talk about." Gina turned to face her daughter. "And it might be best if we do that before people come in. Especially your father."

Marie had hoped to distract her mother from this agenda by revealing the shocking news scoop that David was bringing someone to dinner. And not just any old someone like these creepy boys who occasionally came over "to play," but a female someone. A female someone who was two years older than he was. "And I suppose you know that she's seriously older than he is?" Marie said.

But Gina said, "I want to talk about last night, Marie."

Marie sighed. "What's to talk about?"

"If you can't see that what you did last night was wrong, and not just a little wrong, then maybe you need a lot more disciplining than your father and I thought."

Marie was aware she'd been forced onto the defensive, and she couldn't see a way to avoid dealing with events from the previous night. Oh, well, she'd tried. Time for plan B. "The worst part of last night was upsetting you and Dad so much. But it's not like I was ever really in danger. I mean, I was with the police, right? How much safer can you get?" This was a line of argument suggested by Cassie at school. "But I can see that you and Dad couldn't know nothing was really wrong at first. I mean, when you got the call from the police station, you both must have been really off your twigs."

"We were very upset."

"I am sorry about that, Mum. I really am." And she was. She really was.

"But, that's by no means the only thing that was wrong about last night."

"What else?"

"Can you truly not think of anything else about last night that was not as it should be?"

"Everybody my age drinks, Ma."

Gina said nothing. Her silent stare made Marie seriously uncomfortable.

"And I wasn't supposed to be there alone. Cassie should have come too, but at the last minute she couldn't make it. So there I was with an appointment and no way to call and break it. I didn't want just not to show up—that's not responsible. So my plan was to go to the pub—and it is a public place, after all—my plan was to go and tell him the meeting was off, and then come home. But when I got there, he wasn't there yet. So what could I do? It's not like I could have left a note for him on the door, not in a pub, could I? So I went inside to wait, but I had to buy something. They don't like you just sitting there not drinking anything in a pub, do they? Not that I know much about pubs, but it's a business, isn't it? So I ordered a drink, but then before it came, George arrived, and it was hardly any time after that that everything else happened. So tell me, Mum, just what was I supposed to do?"

Marie was so convinced by the spin on the story as she told it that as she waited for her mother to respond, she lowered her head and began to cry. Then she remembered how she'd felt when she'd been roughly carted off to a police cell. She cried harder.

"Tell me something, Marie."

Marie gulped a couple of times before she said, "What?"

"Just why wasn't Cassie allowed to come to this meeting?"

Uh-oh. Trust her mother to focus on that detail when

149

there was so much else to choose from. Marie sniffled again while she decided whether to argue about the use of the word *allowed*. If she did, Gina might ring Cassie's mother for clarification. Bad. If *that* happened, the whole situation might reel out of control. "I suppose you could say she wasn't 'allowed,' but it wasn't because of George."

However, before Marie could tell her mother what it was because of, David burst into the kitchen. "Hi, Mum!"

"Oh, there you are," Gina said. "David, are you all right?"

"I'm fine."

For once in her life Marie was pleased to see her brother, because it saved her from committing herself as to exactly why Cassie had not been "allowed" out. Nevertheless she glared at him. "Look, it's little Barf-for-Brains, come home at last."

"Shut up, Jail Bird."

"At least I manage not to throw up on myself at school."

"Stop it, both of you," Gina said.

"Mum . . . ," David said. "I've brought home a friend. For dinner." He leaned into the doorway to the landing and beckoned. "That's all right, isn't it?"

Ixy entered the kitchen. "Hi," she said, giving Marie a little wave.

Gina stared at the newcomer, speechless.

David said, "Mum, this is Ixy. Ixy, this is my mother."

Ixy gave Gina a little wave. "Hi."

Gina said, "I . . . I . . . I'm pleased to meet you . . . 'Ixy,' did you say?"

Marie said, "It's short for Victoria. That's what you said

in Drama, isn't it? Her little brother couldn't pronounce Victoria, Mum. Her little brother, who is in David's year."

Mama and the Old Man were on the landing outside the kitchen when Mama took the Old Man's hand.

"What?"

"I can hold my husband's hand if I want, can't I?"

"Huh!" the Old Man said. But Mama felt his squeeze.

She opened the kitchen door. Rosetta was at the cooker stirring the sauce pot, and Gina was by the sink. But sitting at the table there was a young woman. "Who is this?" Mama asked as she walked in.

Gina said, "This is Ixy, Mama."

"Hi," Ixy said, waving at Mama.

"And," Mama said, "you're here for dinner?"

"Yeah. I'm really looking forward to it."

A woman at last . . . "But you're so young."

"I'm sixteen."

"Oh my," Mama said. That made Salvatore . . . how many years older? "Oh my!"

Behind Mama, the Old Man said, "I used to be sixteen."

"Well," Ixy said, "sixteen next birthday."

This, this was a child. And not pretty either. And so red-haired. And an undertaker. What could Salvatore be thinking? Had he gone crazy? Was that it? No woman for months and now this? Mama grasped the back of a kitchen chair.

"Are you all right, Mama?" Gina said.

"Me? I'm not the one who's crazy," Mama said.

"So," the Old Man said, "where is Salvatore?"

"I'm not sure," Gina said, "but he won't be long."

"Huh."

"And how are you, Papa?" Rosetta said.

"Me?" The Old Man considered. "Me, I'm good. And that, what you're cooking, it smells good too."

"Thanks."

"Yes, it does," Ixy said. "And I think it's so great the way you have meals together like this. In my family they all eat in front of the television."

With a deep sigh Mama pulled the chair out and sat herself across from the child. Salvatore should have someone, be settled, of course, that was obvious. And nowadays Mama tried to be flexible. If he didn't want married, well, okay, that could come later. But, but . . . "But isn't sixteen young to have a job? It can't be so wise to leave school."

"School's boring most of the time," Ixy said. "I only like Drama and Media Studies."

"But there's the future to take into account. People always die, of course, but when they die, you bury them, and what else is there? Where can you go with such a job?"

The girl didn't seem to have a ready answer, so maybe the words hit home and now she would reconsider. Salvatore might be disappointed, but it was for the best.

David came into the room.

"Ah, here's my David," the Old Man said.

"Hi, Grandma. Hi, Grandpa. You've met Ixy, then?" David stood behind Ixy's chair.

"We met," Mama said. "We talked about the future, which should always be taken into account."

"Especially if you're an accountant," David said.

Ixy giggled.

"Oh, Mum," David said, "Marie's on the telephone with

Cassie. Is that all right? Because after what happened last night, Dad said that maybe she shouldn't be allowed to talk on the phone again until she was twenty-one."

"Your father and I will decide about all that when he gets home."

"All what?" the Old Man asked. "What is this 'happened last night'?"

"The police took Marie down to the station," David said.

"That's enough, David," Gina said.

"She was drinking in a pub and they thought she was a hooker."

"David!"

"Sorry, Mum."

Rosetta said, "Would somebody like to set the table? Because the food's nearly ready to be served."

Mama said, "Marie was at the police?"

"There was a misunderstanding, Mama," Gina said. "But, yes, last night Marie was with some people who the police took in to ask some questions."

"Not people," David said. "Person. Marie's ex-convict boyfriend."

"Boyfriend?" Mama said. "With Marie there's a boyfriend?"

"No," Gina said. "He's not a boyfriend."

"But last night Dad said you and he are afraid that—"

"That's quite enough misinformation from you, David Lunghi," Gina said. "I'm not going to tell you again."

"And nobody tells us?" the Old Man said. "Not so much as a word?"

"As I said, Papa, it was all a misunderstanding."

"We can't understand a misunderstanding? We can't help

a misunderstanding? Tell me, who here was at the police about a murder? Tell me that. Was it you? Was it Angelo?"

"We just didn't have time to sort ourselves out and do everything we should have," Gina said. "Angelo, Salvatore, and I have been out working all day—as you'll hear at dinner."

"Working on the murder?"

"Yes, and the nine nine nine."

Ixy looked up at David. "A murder? Really?"

"Yeah, a real murder." David put a hand on Ixy's shoulder.

Mama saw the hand. She couldn't believe it.

Gina said, "I don't know what Angelo and Sally have come up with, but there are certainly developments in the nine nine nine."

Mama said, "Nine nine nine emergency? I think *I* should be dialing."

There were footsteps on the stairs.

Rosetta said, "Please, somebody set the table. There are warm plates in the oven."

"David," Gina said. "And perhaps Ixy would like to help you."

"I'd be glad to, Mrs. Lunghi." David's hand fell away as Ixy stood up and moved toward the dining room.

Mama said, "Shouldn't she be here for Salvatore?" but when the kitchen door opened, it was Angelo who came in.

"Sorry I'm late back, but I've been talking with an extra."

"An extra what?" the Old Man asked. He turned to Mama. "Did you hear?"

"I'll explain later, Papa." To Gina Angelo said, "Have you talked to Marie?"

"We started but didn't finish. I got back later than I planned."

"Busy, busy, busy." Angelo sighed.

"I hope they're paying up, these busy-busys," the Old Man said.

"I hope so too, Papa."

"Dad," David said from his place in front of the oven, "meet Ixy."

"Hi, Mr. Lunghi." Ixy waved.

Angelo studied her for a moment. "Do I already know you?"

"How do you know undertakers?" Mama said.

"You look familiar to me," Angelo said.

"What about undertakers?" Rosetta said.

"That's because she's one of the Dirty Girls, Dad," Marie said as she strolled into the kitchen.

"She's what kind of girl?" the Old Man asked.

"They smear horrible things on their faces and look so ugly that people get scared and pay them to go away, Grandpa," Marie said.

"Well, it was your idea, Marie," Ixy said. "And you would have done it too, if you hadn't met a criminal and decided to sell nuts."

"Scare people?" the Old Man said. "Like intimidation?"

"I still can't believe you dippy-dinks took that seriously," Marie said. "All that gunge and gunk. Ugh."

"Marie is exaggerating, Grandpa," David said. "As usual. She wouldn't know the truth if it bit her on the tongue. Unless maybe the police beat it out of her."

"Isn't anybody going to set the table?" Rosetta said. "Because dinner is ready."

"So where is my Salvatore?" Mama asked. "Is he going to leave us alone to entertain his child?"

"What child, Mama?" Gina asked.

But then everybody heard steps on the stairs. There was more than one person.

"Who is that?" Angelo said. "Who are we expecting?"

"Does Salvatore have a child?" the Old Man asked.

Gina said, "That will be Sally."

"And he said he'd probably bring a woman," Rosetta said.

Salvatore entered the kitchen.

"There you are," Mama said. "At last. What are you thinking?"

"Hi, Papa. Hi, everybody." Salvatore bent to kiss Mama on the top of her head. "Sorry if I'm a little late. I hope there's still food because I've brought someone to dinner."

"That I think we already know," Mama said.

"Good. Come on in, Valerie." A woman of about seventy, with silvery hair and dark, bright eyes entered the kitchen. To a silent assemblage Salvatore said, "This is Valerie. She's the Foxwells' neighbor."

"Hello," Valerie said.

"Let's go around the room," Salvatore said. "This is my mother and my father. There's my brother, Angelo, and his wife, Gina. That's their daughter, Marie, and their son, David, and another girl I've never seen before. Hello, girl."

"Hi." Ixy waved.

"And that's my sister, Rosetta. Rose cooks on Thursdays. How close is it all to being ready, Rosie? It smells great. Would you like us to set the table?"

14

*T*his is really quite quite delicious, Rosetta," Valerie said.

"Why thank you," Rosetta said.

"Yeah, it is good, Auntie Rose," David said.

There was general agreement from around the table. "Sometimes I think we're in the wrong business," Salvatore said.

"What wrong business?" the Old Man said. "What 'we'?"

"I think if we set Rosie and Gina up in a little restaurant—and you too, Mama, if you wanted—then they'd be queuing out onto the pavements."

"I don't see anybody starving out on pavements for this wrong business. Huh!"

"But you have to think of the future. Where is the small detective agency going these days, Papa?"

"Future?" the Old Man said. "And I suppose the painting business is so smart for a future?"

"Stop winding him up, Sally," Angelo said.

Gina said, "The restaurant business is not something to

enter lightly." She turned to Valerie. "My family runs restaurants, in Birmingham. So I know whereof I speak."

"Well, if the food in them is anything like this standard, they must be worth a special trip," Valerie said. "Again, Rosetta, it's wonderful, really."

"Look," David said. "Auntie Rose is blushing."

"Even the café business shouldn't be taken lightly," the Old Man said. "Nice if such a person as a macaroni-head knew such a thing." He turned to Mama.

But Mama, who had been silent since Valerie's arrival, had nothing to say.

"What is this pasta, Rosetta?" Valerie said.

"It's *strozza preti,*" Rosetta said.

The Old Man turned to the pasta bowl and spooned some more onto his plate. He said, *"Strozza preti.* You know what it means in English?"

"Sì, li conosco, Valerie said. *"Strozza preti.* 'Strangle the priest,' right?"

"Parla italiano!" the Old Man said.

"Sì, ho vissuto a Verona per ventisei anni."

"Cosa faceva là?"

To David, Marie said, *"Parlez-vous froggais,* empty-*tête?"*

"Mais, oui, merde-visage."

"Yes, all right, you two, enough," Angelo said.

"Perhaps, Papa," Gina said, "you wouldn't mind talking in English while we're at the table."

"Excuse me," Valerie said. "I was being rude. But it is wonderful to use my Italian again. It's a beautiful, beautiful language."

"Una bellissima lingua." Again the Old Man turned to Mama. This time he patted her hand.

Salvatore asked, "What took you to Verona, Valerie?"

"I was married to a sculptor who swore he couldn't live anywhere else, so I was in Verona with him until he died. I expect he's where Paula got her talent from."

"Paula?"

"My daughter. I mentioned her earlier."

"The one who convinced you to make your garden into a nature reserve."

"That's right."

"And Paula is a sculptor?"

"No. A painter. She does night paintings. I don't mean that she paints at night—although she does go out to draw in the dark. I mean that her paintings are of the night. What one would see in the night, as it were."

"Interesting," Salvatore said.

Angelo said, "And she lived with you in the house on High Terrace?"

"That's right. Paula's marriage ended traumatically at about the time my father fell into his final illness. I moved into his house to nurse him and she moved in to nurse me."

"And she too speaks Italian, this painter daughter?" the Old Man said.

"Oh, yes. She spent the first twenty years of her life in Verona."

The Old Man looked at Mama. When she said nothing, he said, "And she's single?"

"She's not married now, but she has a so-called partner, although I'm not sure it's appropriate to call someone a 'partner' who is so envious of her talent that he undermines it at every turn."

"And she lives nearby, this talented painter?" the Old Man asked. He looked at Salvatore.

"They have a house in the country, near Wellow. They've been there for nearly ten years now."

"I'm sorry to have asked about your father and your husband," Angelo said.

"All business for the undertakers," David said. But when everyone turned to him and did not laugh, he said, "Sorry, but I—"

"Shut up, David," Gina said.

"What I was getting at," Angelo said, "was whether your daughter knew the late Phillip Foxwell."

"She did. Mr. Foxwell didn't like it when I let the garden go wild. They had a number of 'conversations' on the subject."

"Conversazione," the Old Man said.

"But it was about then that he disappeared."

"So she was living with you when that happened?"

"Yes, and if you want to talk to her about it, I'll give you her address and phone number."

"Thank you," Angelo said. "I would be very grateful for that."

"Let me do it now, before I forget." Valerie fished in her bag for a pen and wrote the details onto a paper napkin.

The Old Man looked at Mama. After a moment he said, "And this daughter, how old is she?"

"Thirty-six. Why?"

"A good age," the Old Man said. *"Una buona età."*

"Well, I like her." Valerie held up the napkin. "Who . . . ?"

"Salvatore," the Old Man said.

"Sure, why not," Salvatore said.

Valerie said, "It's not every day I can help on a murder case. I'm sure Paula will feel the same way."

"It is a real murder case," the Old Man said. *"E quanti casi di omicidio pensi che abbiamo investigato in tutti questi anni?"*

"I don't know. How many?"

"Solo uno," the Old Man said. "Norman Stiles."

At the name, David and Marie moaned, quickly followed by Rosetta, Salvatore, and Angelo. Ixy giggled and joined in. Valerie sat looking bemused.

"Perhaps our guest would like to hear about Norman Stiles a bit later, Papa," Gina said, "but first I want to ask some questions about the nine nine nine."

Salvatore said to Valerie, "Someone is paging a client of ours and leaving 'Call nine nine nine' messages."

"Oh my."

"Nine nine nine?" Ixy said. "Like for the police or an ambulance or a fire? Ooooo, that's creepy. Sorry. Was it okay for me to say that?"

"Of course," Gina said, "but . . . today our client changed her story."

Suddenly everyone was alert.

"I met her today. First, it turns out that there is some pattern to the nine-nine-nine calls. Weekdays the nine nine nines come at five past the hour."

"Well, well, well," Angelo said.

"Threats on a schedule?" Rosetta said.

"They don't come at every five-past-the-hour. But those that do come on weekdays are at . . ."

Gina conducted as several people said, "Five past the hour."

"And does she only get these nine-nine-nine calls on weekdays?" Salvatore said.

"No. Evenings and weekends the nine nine nines are at random times, as far as the client can tell. I won't use her real name in front of guests. I'll call her Call Me. All right?"

Rosetta said, "But hourly weekdays . . . That's bizarre."

"The whole thing of nine-nine-nine pages is bizarre," Angelo said, "which is why Call Me called us."

"Yes and no," Gina said.

"Oh?" Angelo said. "Something new?"

"While I was talking to her today, I had the feeling that Call Me was holding something back."

"She can pay, this Call Me?" the Old Man asked.

"We'll be paid, Papa."

Angelo said, "She answered what she wasn't telling?"

"Yes. It turns out she doesn't think she's being threatened by a stranger at all."

"Because if she pays, she can hold back whatever she wants," the Old Man said. "And have her funny name. Who cares?"

"She's sure that it is her daughter who is responsible."

All adult eyes turned to Marie, who was picking absently at her pasta. When she became aware of the silence, she looked up. "What?"

"She said a daughter?" the Old Man said.

"Yes, Papa," Gina said.

Angelo said, "But why didn't Call Me say so when she originally came to us?"

"You tell me." Gina spread her hands, palms up, a gesture that invited general speculation.

"She didn't know it was her daughter when she came?" Rosetta said.

When Gina shook her head. "She feared her daughter was responsible all along."

"Yet allowed us to theorize that she's being threatened by a stranger," Salvatore said. "Interesting."

"A male stranger," Angelo said.

"So, she doesn't really want us to stop the nine nine nines."

"Or she doesn't care whether we do or not," Gina said.

"But why come to us?" Salvatore said.

Valerie said, "May I ask something? Is that all right?"

"Of course," Gina said.

"Was it Call Me's own idea to come to you in the first place?"

Gina clapped. "Excellent. Correct. It was not *her* idea to come to us."

"So whose?" Then Angelo nodded. "Ah, the boyfriend."

"Call Me received some of the nine-nine-nine pages while she and her boyfriend were together," Gina said.

"But he bought the pager," Angelo said. "So he asks, 'Who's paging you?' She says, 'I don't know.' So he wants to see the pager messages."

"But when he sees the nine nine nines, he says, 'That's a threat. You have to do something about it.'"

"And we are what she did," Angelo said. "Well, well, well."

Gina said, "She was genuinely scared, but mostly because she sensed her daughter's involvement."

Salvatore said, "So do we still have a case?"

"We still have a case, because the nine nine nines are still coming," Gina said.

"Does Call Me want us to 'catch' the daughter?"

"She wants us to stop the nine nine nines."

"Why doesn't she speak to her daughter?" Valerie said.

"The truth of it," Gina said, "is that she's afraid of her daughter."

"Afraid? What of?"

"The daughter is one of those 'different' children. Which means different from her mother. She's always liked spiders and rats, where Call Me expected a daughter to be clean and frilly. Call Me feels that she and her daughter are almost from different planets."

"So those stories about what aliens do—"

"Thank you, David," Gina said.

"Is she worried about the daughter knowing she has a boyfriend?" Salvatore said.

"I'm sure that's part of it."

"How old is this daughter?" the Old Man said.

"Good question, Papa. She's seventeen, in her second A-level year." Gina turned to the children. "Not at your school, or I'd have sent you out of the room before we started talking."

Marie said, "May I be excused?"

"Why?"

"I need to call Cassie."

Angelo said, "Talk to her at school."

"It's about homework."

"Do your own homework."

"It's me who helps her, Daddy. And before you say, 'Tell her to do her own homework,' it's for Drama and we've been assigned to do projects in pairs. If you don't believe me, just ask Ixy. She's in the same class."

Eyes turned to Ixy, who cleared her throat and said, "That's right, Mr. Lunghi."

Marie said, "But I'll stay at the table if you want me to fail Drama. It's entirely up to you."

Angelo rubbed his eyes. It was clear to everyone he didn't know what to say. Gina said, "Stay here."

"Mum!"

"You heard your mother," Angelo said. "You can re-take."

Marie sank back into her seat.

"So," Salvatore said, "we have an A-level student whose mother thinks she's behind nuisance pages. Did the mother give the girl her pager number?"

"No," Gina said.

"So how did she get it?"

"You tell me." When nobody spoke, Gina said, "Marie?"

Without looking up Marie said, "The daughter went through the mother's bag and found it?"

"That was my first thought too," Gina said, "but when I asked, Call Me said that the only number she carries is for her boyfriend's pager."

David said, "Maybe she hacked into the system and got the number that way."

"Trust you to think of the geek-head solution," Marie said.

"As it happens," Gina said, "David might be right."

David stuck his tongue out at Marie. Marie poked at it with her fork.

"Because this particular daughter is a high-flying scientist. But, she is not good at maths. And that's something I wanted to ask. Can you hack into computers without being good at maths? What do you think? Rose? David?"

"The kids I know who hack are all good at maths too," David said.

"He's admitting he hacks, Mum," Marie said. "I hope you're going to punish him for that."

Rosetta said, "There's something . . ." But she stopped.

"What, Rose?" Gina asked.

Rosetta shook her head. "Nothing. Sorry." She glanced at David.

Valerie said, "I've been thinking about something else. May I . . . ?" Gina nodded. "However this girl got the pager number, aren't the weekdays at five past the hour significant? Mightn't they fit with her school schedule?"

"Ah," Salvatore said, "she nine-nine-nines between classes. Good. You're not just a pretty face." He patted Valerie's hand.

"And easy to check," Angelo said. "Is that what you do next? Call the school to see if the class breaks fit these nine nine nines?"

"I already did," Gina said.

"And?"

"And they don't. All through the day at five past the hour students at the school would be in classes."

"Oh," Angelo said.

"So, what now, what next? That's my question."

Mama sat up straight in her chair. "I have a question."

"Good, Mama," Gina said.

"I want to know," Mama said, "just who, exactly, is the undertaker?"

"What?"

"Who is the undertaker? That I want to know. It's the least that my Salvatore could tell me."

"I don't know what you're talking about, Mama," Salvatore said.

"I do," Rosetta said.

All eyes turned to her.

"My Christopher is an undertaker. Although he may become a line-dance teacher. He hasn't decided yet."

15

When Salvatore and Valerie arrived at Valerie's door on High Terrace, she said, "Thanks again for inviting me to dinner. I enjoyed it."

"Good. I enjoyed your being there," Salvatore said. And it was true. Which surprised him, given that he'd made the invitation solely as a device to get Mama off his back.

"Do you think your mother will be all right?" Valerie said.

"She just got herself confused, and it upset her. She'll be back on her own track by tomorrow, if not before."

"I hope so."

Salvatore heard what he took for doubt in her voice. "Do you think she won't be?"

"You know her far better than I do, so I'm sure you're right. But my father's decline began with episodes of confusion and anger, so . . ." Valerie stopped. She looked away.

"I'm sorry about your father." A light on the lane reflected off Valerie's hair and made the waves in it look snowy. Salvatore felt an impulse to touch it. But he resisted.

Valerie said, "I was just remembering something Paula

168

says, that my experience with my father predisposes me to see the same pattern in other people even when it's not appropriate. It's come up a few times, even once with her boyfriend. In fact that was part of why she moved away when she did—though in his particular case I'm not sure my predisposition wasn't more correct than she realized. But parents always fret about their children. We're afraid they will make needless mistakes."

"My mother would agree with you there."

"You don't have children?"

"No," Salvatore said.

"There's time."

"I hope so."

"Look, would you like to come in for a cup of coffee?"

After a moment Salvatore said, "Sure. Why not."

"I'd invite you in," Ixy said, "but it's already late for a school night."

"No problem." But David's heart was beating. He didn't know whether not being invited in also meant that he shouldn't kiss her. Was the doorstep "in" or "out"? And what about the fact they'd held hands all the way back to Ixy's house after dinner. Did that change things?

"I think your family's so cool."

"Yeah. Except Marie."

"She does think a lot of herself."

David wasn't sure he agreed with that assessment. Marie just didn't like being told what to do. But would disagreeing with Ixy about the subject mean they would talk about Marie instead of kiss? And should he be moving closer to her? "Yeah."

He was about to step forward when Ixy said, "And you're not like any boy I've ever met before either."

"You make me sound like I'm from another planet."

"I mean it in a good way. Other boys, you say hello to them and they're pawing you. But you're so . . . restrained."

David didn't feel restrained. And he didn't like the image of other boys pawing Ixy. He lifted his hands in front of his chest and said, "Paw, paw." Being careful not to let his hands get anywhere near her chest. Ixy's chest. What a thought. He felt blood rising to his face. He hoped she couldn't see.

But she just laughed.

"Paw, paw," he said, but he felt stupid for saying it again. What should he do?

Then behind Ixy the front door opened. A soft-faced boy with red hair leaned out. "Dad says to stop snogging and come in. Oh, hi, David. I didn't realize it was you."

"Hi, Scottie," David said.

"I don't believe Daddy said anything at all," Ixy said. "You're just snooping. Go back to your dolls."

"Last night it was so cool," Scottie said. "I got into somebody's personal files. Diary, spreadsheet, clothing sizes, all kinds of stuff."

"Yeah?" David said.

"The password is just the last name spelled backwards. It's pretty clever if I do say so myself. Do you want to see?"

For just a moment David considered saying yes.

"Oh, brilliant," Ixy said. She pushed her brother into the house and followed him in, leaving David on the stoop facing the closed door with both hands in front of his chest.

Mama was mumbling.

"Tea? You want tea?" the Old Man asked. He could make tea. It came in bags, right? You boil water.

But Mama just said, "Why do they do this?"

"What?"

She didn't answer. Was she going to be like that all evening? He didn't know what to do.

She mumbled again. He couldn't make out what.

"What?"

She stopped mumbling, but she didn't respond. She just sat in her chair looking into space.

"What?" he said again.

She sat motionless, so still that for an instant he was worried. What if . . . He went to her side, knelt, and took her hand. It was warm.

She turned to face him. "Again?"

"What?"

She squeezed his hand. Then he saw she was crying.

"What?"

"Old woman," she said.

What was this? She never called herself such a thing. She wasn't such a thing. She was the same as when she had stepped off the boat. A light, airy creature who could barely keep her feet on the ground. A dancing girl who skipped down the gangplank. The Old Man felt something in his own eyes.

Mama said, "If he marries that old woman, he'll never have children."

As silently as she could, Marie opened the door to her room. When the gap was just wide enough to slip through, she stood by it and listened, trying to hear who was where in the rest of the flat. Rather disappointingly, she heard nothing that she could interpret. But perhaps the silence meant everyone was home and in his or her own rooms.

In particular she strained to hear the click and tap of David at work on his computer, his usual night sound. But she heard nothing.

Oh, well, nothing ventured . . . Stealthily Marie moved into the hall toward the telephone table that stood against the opposite wall. She picked the telephone up, carried the prize back into her room, and closed the door. She could tell no one else was on the phone because a light would show it. But in the same way, phones elsewhere would light as she used this one. She would have to be fast.

After a breath, Marie picked up the receiver. She dialed Cassie's number. It rang. And rang again. But after the fourth ring it was answered. And it was Cassie.

"Hi," Marie said.

"Hey! You're alive," Cassie said. "I thought they grounded you for the rest of your life with no telephone and only bread and water."

"They only give me bread if I'm good."

Cassie giggled. Then Marie heard a voice behind Cassie but close enough to be clear: "It's too late for phone calls, Cassandra."

"I can't talk."

"Me neither," Marie said. "I'm dead meat if they catch me. Look, I told them we're doing a Drama project together, one that has to be done in twos. Tell your mum the same in case they call her. Okay?"

Gently Marie returned the telephone receiver to its cradle.

Then, still making efforts to be quiet, she carried the phone back into the hall. But before she could replace it on its table, David appeared. Damn! He was bound to threaten to tell their parents that she'd been on the phone when she'd been specifically told at the table that she should fail Drama instead of calling Cassie. Could she claim to have called someone else? Or was there something she could offer him to buy his silence?

But David said nothing. He passed by Marie in the hall and went toward his room. What was that about? Ah, he'd walked Ixy home.

"Is that lipstick on your collar, or gunge?" It was out before she could control it. She regretted it instantly.

Without looking back David said, "Shut your *bouche,* rabbit head, or I'll tell about the phone." He disappeared into his room.

As Angelo slipped into bed, he said, "Do you think Mama will be all right?"

"I should think so," Gina said. "She just got confused."

"We all get confused. She seemed upset."

"She needs Sally and Rose to bring their friends to dinner so she can keep things straight."

"Did you know about Christopher being an undertaker?"

"No," Gina said.

"Was she hiding it?"

"Maybe."

"She said he didn't come to dinner because he works nights and goes to see his own mother on Sundays." After a moment Angelo said, "What does an undertaker do at night?"

"Suck out the blood?"

"Charming. I always wondered where David and Marie got it from."

"What do we do about Marie?" Gina said. "We can't leave it much longer if we're going to 'do' anything."

"I don't want to do anything about it," Angelo said, "except make sure that for the rest of her life she only leaves the house when she's manacled to one of us."

"And your second choice?"

"I thought you were going to talk to her. Get her to say how to punish her."

"I began before dinner but we were interrupted, and after dinner . . ."

"There was no chance. Well, maybe tomorrow."

"I think it may be too late."

"Why?"

"She'll have her whole story too well rehearsed."

Angelo frowned. "What do you mean?"

"The time to catch liars is before they get their story straight, before they iron out their stumbles."

"So are you're saying Marie lies to us?"

"Of course she lies to us," Gina said.

"I don't like that," Angelo said. "It's not right."

"Did you ever lie to your parents?"

Angelo paused. "That was different."

"That was the same, except that this time she got involved with the police."

"I would have been petrified if the police took me in when I was her age."

"I'm sure it scared her."

"She doesn't act it."

"She takes Drama," Gina said. "She wouldn't want to admit."

"So there is a problem or there isn't a problem? I don't understand."

"Marie behaved badly and lied to us, but the worst part is that she didn't recognize that she was getting herself into danger. Suppose the police hadn't come. Suppose she had agreed to sell nuts for this George Skillman idiot. She would have handled the stolen goods, a crime. And that's even if he didn't use the situation to try to take sexual advantage."

Sexual advantage? Oh, dear, Angelo thought.

"But Marie did not realize the danger," Gina said.

"Does she recognize it now?"

"Probably."

"Probably." Angelo sighed. "Probably, probably. Who would be a parent?"

"I think the lecture she got at the police station did it better than we could have."

"Probably."

"But I also think we have to consider what to do about the reason she was involved in all this in the first place."

"Money. She wants money. So she should save." But before Gina could respond Angelo said, "She can't. I know. I know. So what do we do?"

"That's the problem. How do we find a way for her to earn money without it being a reward for behaving recklessly?"

"Buy her a lottery ticket? It worked for Winston Foxwell." When Gina was silent, Angelo said, "But I think the manacles are better."

. . .

David was lying on his bed with his head beneath his pillow when there was a light tapping on his door. Marie, coming to torture him. "Go away." he said. Then louder, "Go away!"

But when the door opened, he heard Rosetta say, "I couldn't hear what you said. I hope it's okay to come in."

David rolled up, leaning against the wall. He didn't really want to talk to anyone, but at least Auntie Rose wasn't Marie. "Hi."

"What are you doing under there?"

David considered offering something fanciful. Looking for minute Martians? But he didn't feel like it. "Just thinking."

"I thought you'd be at your computer."

David looked at the blank screen. It represented the source of his misery. Ixy hated computers. "I don't feel like it. In fact, I don't know if I'll ever turn it on again."

Rosetta frowned. "Because it's your computer I want to talk about."

"What?"

Rosetta turned his computer chair to face the bed and sat on it. "You've been hacking into the agency files at night, haven't you?"

What? Oh. "Have I?"

"I can tell, David. It shows when someone's been in and at what time. I see it when I go to the files to write the invoices. Like, a couple of nights ago, you opened the Celia Corman file."

"The what?"

"The one your parents call the Dirty Girls."

"Oh."

"What are you doing in the files?"

"Just reading them. And . . ."

"And what?"

"And sometimes I work on the cases."

"You what?"

"I go to places and see the people we're working for."

"But why?"

"In case I can find out something to help. And that case, the Corman, that was a breakthrough. I went to where Dad was paying them off and it turned out I knew them. And now I know a lot about the Dirty Girls that Mum and Dad don't know. I know who they all are, which shops they've been going to, and what their schedule is. And I know how much money they've been making. Dad didn't get any of that."

"But how did . . . ? Oh. The girl at dinner."

"Yes."

"Ixy. That's her name isn't it?"

"Yes."

"But I thought she was your girlfriend."

"She is. I mean, I think she is. I . . ." Oh, Ixy! David felt tears welling up in his eyes, but before he could do anything to stop them, they were pouring out, onto his cheeks.

"David!" Rosetta put her arms around him. He clung to her.

"Oh, Auntie Rose! When she went in, she didn't say good-night. I just don't know what to do!"

"You're late," Heather said.

"Yes," Salvatore said.

"Well?"

"Well what? Is there a problem?"

Heather laughed. "We're not married, Salvatore." She crossed herself. "We're not even a 'couple.' "

177

"We're not?"

"Not if it implies you can't stay out late if you want to. When you left, you didn't say, 'I'll be back at such and such a time.' So, no contract was broken."

"But you said I was late."

"Your reaction tells me more about the women who have preceded me than your words ever have. It was an observation inviting discussion, Salvatore. Not a criticism. Perhaps something of special interest took place. Something you'd like to share with me."

"Ah."

"You're just back a lot later than when you've gone to your family meals before."

"Yes."

Heather laughed again.

Salvatore felt slightly annoyed. "What?" When she didn't answer, he said, "You should come sometime."

"We've been through all that. I won't lie to them."

"I never asked you to lie."

"But you did say—"

"I know what I said. It's just my mother gets upset. She got upset tonight. It's a good example. It came out that my sister's boyfriend is an undertaker. She kind of went off the deep end. Papa had to take her back upstairs."

With some effort Heather eased off the mattress and got to her feet. She pressed closed to Salvatore and said, "And it upset you too. I am sorry, honey." She surrounded him with her arms, then hooked a leg behind his knee. With one of her hands she held the back of his head. She licked his neck, his cheek, his ear, his forehead.

And Salvatore's annoyance vanished. There was something about her hands, her touch, her lick. Slowly his arms found their way around her body.

"And I bet I could help your mother too, if you want me to try."

The image of Heather "healing" his mother was too powerful for Salvatore not to respond to. He chuckled.

"*You* feel better now, don't you?" Heather said quietly.

"Yes. Would you hug her too?"

"If I thought it would work, but first—"

"I don't even want to think about that. So what have you been up to this evening?"

Heather dropped her leg back to the floor and stood back. "I sorted some things out with Running Bear and Nasrullah."

"You're actually going to do it, then?"

"Yes."

"There are enough of you?"

"We went through the people each of us knows. Put us together and we have a lot to offer. We're going to start looking for a place."

"And money?"

"Something will come up."

"I'll pay you for modeling for the paintings I want to do." Heather laughed.

"But if we're not a couple, I ought to pay for modeling."

"Sally, honey, when you draw me or paint me, it's sex for you. I won't take money from you for that. Even if you do come home late smelling of another woman's perfume."

"But I thought love was supposed to be a good thing," David said.

He looked so sad. Rosetta's heart went out to him and

she put her arms around him and patted his back. "Of course it's a good thing. It's the best thing."

"It is? So why do I feel like *this?*" He buried his face in his hands.

"Love *is* good, but it's hard. And it's hard because it involves another person, and you can't always tell what that person is thinking or feeling."

"But how do you find out what she's thinking or feeling?"

Rosetta was about to suggest that he could ask when her nephew turned to her and said, "Are you in love with your undertaker, Auntie Rose?"

"With Christopher? Uh, well, I'm not really sure."

"But you've been in love before, haven't you? You were with Walter, weren't you?"

Walter. That slime.

"Weren't you?" David persisted.

"I thought I was, but I wasn't."

David sighed deeply. "If someone as old as you doesn't know, what hope is there for me?"

"It doesn't really work like a computer, David. It's not something you know is there just by looking to see if the screen is lit up."

"Oh." David thought some more. "Do you get miserable about Christopher?"

"No. Well, not so far."

"But you will?"

"I . . . I don't know. I hope not, but I suppose it could happen."

"Did you get miserable about Walter?"

That scum. Amazing to have spent years with a man but

now to think about him so rarely that when he's mentioned, he sounds like some stranger.

"Auntie Rose?"

"I did get miserable with Walter. At the end."

"At the end? The *end*? But I've only been with Ixy for a *day*."

Rosetta hugged him and pulled him close again. "It will be all right, David. It doesn't have to be the end. You can feel miserable any old time when you're in love."

David clung to her. "Auntie Rose, I feel so scared."

Rosetta wondered if she should feel scared too.

16

In the morning, everything felt rushed to Gina. Marie not appearing until the last minute was common enough—and given the current circumstances, to be expected. But today even David was late.

"Where's your brother?" Gina asked Marie.

"Cooling his banana."

"What?"

"I don't know, Mum. Do I look like a zookeeper?" Marie picked up an apple and hunted on the floor beneath the coats for her schoolbag.

"David," Gina called, but as she did so, he appeared. He looked a mess. His hair wasn't combed and his school shirt was buttoned wrongly. "Are you going to school like that?"

"Like what?"

Marie looked up and said, "Love's young dream."

"If you're going to squat, shouldn't you do it outside?" David said.

"That's enough of that," Gina said. "Are you all right, David?"

"No," he said with a snarl. "I'm all left." He grabbed a banana, and then his coat, kneeing Marie in the process. "Come on, horse-face. Time we 'left.' You can get some hay on the way."

David pushed through the kitchen door, forcing Angelo, who was coming in, to step back. Newspaper in hand, Angelo stepped toward the door again only to be shoved aside once more by Marie.

"What was that?" Angelo asked when he did finally achieve the kitchen.

"The beginning of David-the-adolescent," Gina said with a sigh. "He sounded just like Marie two years ago."

Angelo sat down. "I think I'm going to call in sick. Take a couple of years off."

"Start tomorrow. We're too busy today."

Angelo opened the newspaper. "Maybe today they announce the adolescence pill." He turned a page. As he did so, Mama appeared.

"Morning, Mama. Would you like a cup of tea?" Gina said.

"It's not tea I want."

The harsh edge to Mama's voice made both Gina and Angelo stop what they were doing and look at her. "What can we get you?" Gina said lightly.

"Salvatore you can get me."

"What do you mean?" Angelo said.

"You don't understand what means *Salvatore?* Your own brother?"

"Well," Angelo said uncertainly, "Sally's not here."

"That I see for myself. And neither does he answer his telephone. What must I do? Hire a detective?"

"You phoned Salvatore at this time in the morning?" Gina said. What she had in mind was to try to lighten the tone of the conversation. Her brother-in-law was well known within the family for his late nights and his late mornings.

But Mama would not be lightened. "At this time, I'm talking to you. Five minutes ago I telephoned Salvatore. And fifteen minutes before that. And fifteen minutes before that. So, where is he?"

"I don't know. Do you know, Gina?"

"No."

"That's it?" Mama said. "That's all?"

"If he's not at his flat, we don't know where he might be," Gina said.

"So, to find him I must hire. Perhaps you can recommend a detective." But instead of waiting for a recommendation, or further conversation, Mama turned and left the kitchen. She slammed the door behind her.

"I've heard of second childhood," Angelo said, "but second adolescence?"

The Old Man sat with his hands around a cup of coffee. The television was on, but with no sound. Watching the breakfast people bob around on their sofas, smiling flight-attendant smiles and being playful with each other, made him laugh with the sound off. With the sound on, he never laughed.

Behind him, Mama entered the flat. Her, she made noise. "So, was he there, Salvatore?"

"What do you think?"

"I think Mussolini was stupid to side with the Germans," the Old Man said. "What do you mean, what do I think?"

"He wasn't there. He's nowhere. My oldest son, who I

was in painful labor with for eleven hours, he's vanished, that's what they say."

"So where is he?"

"What, is my sound off too? You don't listen? They don't know. Nobody knows."

"Somebody knows," the Old Man said. "Salvatore knows. And if he'd given up the stupid painting, then he'd be in his room downstairs. You'd only have to knock."

"I need a detective," Mama said.

"What?" The statement surprised him. The Old Man decided to turn the television off. Instead he hit the mute button.

The television roared, a woman's voice, saying, "... took swabs from under their armpits and dissolved them in alcohol. Then we dabbed some of the solution on the upper lips of our volunteers and . . ." The Old Man found the power button and killed the set.

"What?" he said again. "You need what?"

"A detective. Do you know one for hire? Downstairs they can't help."

What was this about? "What do you want a detective for?"

"To find my son, of course."

"He's missing?"

"I'm missing him. So, can you find my son for me, old man?"

"Me?"

"I thought you were a detective. That's what my husband tells me all these years. Perhaps he lies."

"Of course I'm a detective," the Old Man said solemnly.

"So I want to hire, to find my son. And don't ask which son—I know you. Find Salvatore. Can you do it?"

185

"Of course I can do it. But can you pay?"

When Angelo came up to the office after unlocking the downstairs door, Gina was already at her desk. "What time is Call Me Esta?"

"I told her ten."

"Did she come on time before?"

"Not far off, but either way it's a busy day. What is the post?"

Angelo passed her the pile of envelopes. "Remind me of the busy. Esta and . . . ?"

"Salvatore said he would visit Paula the daughter this morning."

"Daughter? Oh. Of the woman last night. I liked her. What was . . ."

"Valerie."

"Right. The Foxwell neighbor. And a daughter who lived there at the disappearance." Something else was known about the daughter. It didn't come to mind immediately. I'm getting old, Angelo thought. Maybe not getting sleep young predicts what it feels like old. But then what he was trying to remember came to him. "This daughter, she's a painter?"

Gina leaned back and smiled. "You're matchmaking."

"I am?" Oh, Salvatore to visit the daughter painter.

"Like Papa was last night."

He was? "But isn't Salvatore with the mother? Valerie."
Gina sighed audibly.

"What?" Angelo said.

"It doesn't matter." Picking up the post, Gina said, "The daughter has a boyfriend anyway. A 'partner' at least."

Ah, yes. Jealous of the talent. "So, Sally at the painter. Esta here. What else?"

"I have to go to Winston Foxwell's wife. She wouldn't talk to Sally yesterday."

"No?"

"She won't talk to a man. And we need to know if she knew Uncle Foxwell, have a look inside the house, and get a general idea of her."

"So I am left with Call Me Esta?"

"Do you mind?" Gina said.

She had a smile. What did it mean? Angelo frowned. "And what do I want from Call Me Esta again?"

"Tell her the five-past-the-hours don't fit Susan, the daughter."

"Does she have any other children? Maybe it's one of them."

"Ask," Gina said. "Otherwise, next we need to talk to the daughter."

"Shouldn't she be the one to talk to her daughter?"

"She won't."

"She won't talk to her own daughter?"

Gina put down the envelope she had just opened and stared across the room.

"Sorry. Sorry. Sorry. I'm slow today." Angelo scratched his head. "So, is there time for tea, this busy day?"

Since he was working on a case, the Old Man went out not long after he finished a second cup of breakfast coffee. He headed for Lansdown Hill.

Salvatore was going to talk to a Paula this morning. Paula, the daughter of last night's too-old woman. The neighbor of the Foxwell client, whose address at 7 High Terrace was written down when he first opened this murder case. Paula's address too was written down, last night on a serviette by the woman, this Paula's mother. She gave it to Salvatore.

They thought he didn't remember such things. They thought he didn't pay attention. But he knew. Not so much slipped past.

Although it was a cold day, the sun was shining. The heavy coat was right, but so was walking up Lansdown Hill to the High Terrace. No point running up the client's bill with needless taxis. Some might do that, but not him.

This mother of the daughter was a neighbor of 7 High Terrace, so 6 or 8. Or maybe 5 or 9 if the Terrace was odd. But they would know a woman with a Paula, someone near. Ask and they would tell. If not the first, then the second. People like to tell. A basic fact that makes it possible to detect. Detective is asking, mostly. Huh.

When High Terrace was not quite where the Old Man thought it would be, he asked for it. Then High Terrace was there after all, and just as well to have walked because cars didn't drive.

After standing at the end of the lane to catch his breath, the Old Man walked to Number 7. A modest Bath stone house. The pointing was in good condition, and there was expensive double-glazing. The roofline was good.

Could Angelo or Salvatore make such an assessment? Sometimes they forgot he did more than set up an agency, from nothing. He bought property. Solid property, good buildings, no rot, and sound roofs. Not easy to find adjoining, but now everyone benefited, even if they ignored.

Yes, Number 7 was good. But Number 6, such chaos in

the front garden! As if no one lived, except in the windows upstairs there were curtains. So an old person, or a poor one. But poor can keep a garden tidy. How expensive to cut down dead weeds? Even in December these were waist height and bowing from their own weight toward the earth as if they longed to join it.

But no rubbish among the stooping weeds. An old person, probably. But wouldn't some neighbor help out? The other gardens on the lane were tidy. How much trouble to mow a little patch? Surprising that such tidy neighbors don't demand about the mess, make a fuss. So, an old person in Number 6 who fights neighbors, go away and mind your own business. Huh.

So this Number 6 could not be the mother of the Paula. The mother last night looked nice, talked to people, spoke well. So the Old Man turned away from Number 6, walked up the path to Number 8, and knocked on the door.

When Gina left the office, Angelo stood in the window above the street and watched her emerge onto the pavement. He saw her pull her coat tight and then toss her hair before she wrapped it in a scarf. As she looked each way before crossing the street, he looked each way too.

Once she was on the other side, she headed for a gap between the buildings that was the shortcut up to the London Road. Swiftly she passed out of sight into the dark hole, and as she did so, Angelo felt a soft moment of loss, of missing her. For just a moment he wondered if he would ever see her again.

"Stupid man," he said aloud. He rustled the leaves of the scented-leaved pelargoniums on the sill beneath the window, and he intended to leave his post and get on with the day.

But instead of gathering the mugs to rinse, he stayed at the window. The "soft" moment had passed its peak of intensity, but still Angelo was particularly aware of Gina. She understood people so much better than he did. He would make so many mistakes if she didn't redirect him. What would he do if . . .

"Stupid man," he said again. "Oxymoron?" Then, "Dumb oxymoron."

At last he left the window and stepped away. He took the tea mugs to the sink in the little office bathroom and scrubbed them with a brush. Would Salvatore ever know what it was like to have a Gina in his life? If not, he would be missing out.

When Salvatore awoke, it was to Heather's tongue darting over his face. "Hey, what's this about?" he said with a smile. He slipped an arm around her waist.

"I just wanted to make sure that the good work of last night wasn't lost. Okay?"

Salvatore closed his eyes and concentrated on the tiny touches. He couldn't always tell where her tongue was or what it was doing, but the net result was soothing, no doubt about it. The woman soothed him like no other.

Then, for a time, Heather drew patterns and blew gently on the bits of skin she had wetted. She made patterns on his forehead and around his eyes. Then she made different patterns on the underside of his chin. Always her touch was delicate and moist.

She was something else, this Heather. What on earth was

he going to do about her? Of course that was by no means entirely his decision.

When Salvatore finally realized that she had stopped, Heather was already inches away from him and gazing into his eyes. There it was again, her Mona Lisa. Painting her was a necessity. Anything else would wait until after.

"Okay?" she asked.

"Linguini."

"What?"

" 'Little tongues.' That's what it means. As my father would be sure to tell you if . . . Oops, sorry. Wrong subject."

"There's no subject that's wrong, honey. And if you'd like me to meet your family, we can talk about it."

"You don't know what you'd be getting into."

"I have a family," Heather said. "And they don't like what I do any more than yours likes what you do."

"My mother was amazing last night. She went for ages without saying a word."

"I'm sorry she's not well. Do you know what's wrong with her?"

Salvatore took a deep breath. "They tell me it's because she thinks I've given up women."

"Little does she know." Salvatore was about to say something but she put a finger on his lips. "But how does that make her unwell?"

"She wants me to settle down. But she thinks I've stopped trying to find Ms Right." He spread his hands. "Or so I am told."

Heather was silent for a moment. "It's not for me to tell you what to do, honey."

191

"I don't like to upset Mama, but for you to meet my mother would not just be your meeting her. Nothing is ever enough. That's the thing about my mother, it's never enough until she gets her way, and what she wants is for me to get married."

"Is that a proposal?"

"What?"

"Your face," Heather said with a laugh as she eased herself to her knees. She rocked to her feet. "Maybe I should paint it."

When Gina knocked lightly at Number 7 High Terrace, the door opened a crack almost immediately. The face inside was hard to make out in the shadow. "Mrs. Foxwell?"

The gap opened wider, illuminating a small, pale female head. The woman didn't speak. She just stared at Gina.

"Are you Mrs. Sheila Foxwell?"

"Who wants to know?"

"My name is Gina Lunghi. I'm an investigator and I believe a colleague of mine spoke to you briefly yesterday, but you didn't want to talk to him."

"Oh, are you the woman? A man stood there yesterday, said he'd send a woman. Said he was hired to help Winston."

"That's right."

"You're hired too? 'Hired'? As in money?"

"Yes."

"But that's expensive, ain't it? Who in the world would pay money to help Winston? Certainly not that cow of a mother of his. She'd never pay for anything useful, like getting her kid out of jail so he could look after his family."

"My understanding is that Mr. Foxwell is paying."

"What Mr. Foxwell? There's none of them left that I've heard of. His dad was drunk and walked in front of a moped. And now his uncle, dead in the garden." The woman peered narrowly at Gina again. "Unless it was that old man who was looking at the house a little while ago. Stood looking for a long time. What's he, then, somebody's father or something? Long lost? Like on the telly? Wants to pay for past wrongs? Like that *Our Mutual Fund* by Charles Dickson, in all them epicsodes? Is that it?"

"I don't know anything about an old man looking at your house. The Mr. Foxwell I mean is Winston Foxwell, your husband."

"Winston? Pay? With what?" Sheila Foxwell peered harder at Gina. "If he's got money, he's been holding out on me and little Phil."

The woman's look was so fierce Gina wondered if her husband might not be wiser to stay where he was. "Payment for my agency's work is being handled through a solicitor, Mrs. Foxwell. But no matter who's paying, if I'm going to help your husband, I need to talk to you."

"What about?"

"Your history in this house. Whether you knew your husband's uncle."

"Never. He was long gone before I even met Winston." Sheila Foxwell looked thoughtful. "Everything that needed to be done, Winston found the necessary. Said it fell off a lorry. And I believed him. I'm such a fool."

"May I come in, please, Mrs. Foxwell?"

"I suppose. But if you want tea, it'll be with a used tea bag. That's how things stand with me. Everything I get goes to little Phil."

"Little Phil would be your son?"

"Yeah." Sheila Foxwell nodded vaguely toward the interior of the house. Then she stepped back from the door and waved Gina in, saying, "You'd think his nana would stump up for her only grandchild, but she doesn't, except dumb plastic toys and battery crap. He could go out in rags in the winter, for all the old bat cares. He could go hungry like that *Oliva Twits* by Charles Dickson she was so proud of, standing next to the porridge pot on the telly."

Gina followed Sheila Foxwell through a dark hallway to a kitchen at the back.

"What the hell, I'll put the kettle on. You'd be surprised how far a tea bag will go if you try."

Esta Dumphy did not arrive until well past ten-thirty, and when she did, she was not alone. Jerry Northam followed her into the office. Neither of them was smiling.

Hello, hello, hello, what have we here? Angelo thought. Trouble in paradise? "Good morning. Nice to see you again, Mr. Northam."

"Let's dispense with the chitchat if you don't mind," Northam said. "We just want to get this matter settled as fast as we can, don't we?"

Angelo looked to Esta, but she said nothing. "We'd all like that, I think," Angelo said. He gestured for them to use the settee.

The couple settled and Angelo sat facing them. Northam said, "Now, about Susan. Esta's daughter."

"You think she may have something to do with the nine nine nines, don't you, Mrs. Dumphy?" Angelo said.

"It was just a feeling." Esta glanced at Northam. "There

was nothing specific." She seemed a different woman today. Meek, colorless, not special.

"I think this five-past-the-hour business is pretty specific." Shaking his head slowly, Northam said, "I only heard about that last night."

Angelo said, "The question is, what does five past the hour mean?"

"I should think that was obvious," Northam said.

"Not if you're trying to connect it to Susan," Angelo said. "It turns out that Susan is in class at five past the hour throughout the entire school day."

"What?"

Esta fixed her eyes on Angelo's face as he said, "We managed to establish that yesterday. There is no way that Susan could be making calls to the pager at that time. Well, not unless she truants regularly. Does she skip school, Mrs. Dumphy?"

"No. Never." There was new life in her expression.

"So"—Angelo spread his hands—"your mystery caller is not Susan."

"But if she isn't making the damn calls, who is?" Northam said.

"I think that's what you and Mrs. Dumphy hired us to find out in the first place, isn't it?"

"First your charming son and now you," Valerie said. "It seems to be my week for handsome men." She led the Old Man into her living room.

"It's not my intention to bother you like Salvatore, but I need to ask a favor."

"Ask away. *Intanto, voule un caffe?*"

The Old Man took a moment before saying, *"Sì, grazie."* There was no need to charge the client for time with the coffee. Besides, sometimes sociability can get better cooperation.

Valerie left the Old Man in the living room and he went to the front window. Through the weeds in the front garden he could see the city in the valley below. The view would be good if the garden were even ordinarily tidy. People paid fortunes for such views. And upstairs the panorama would be exceptional.

"The coffee will be ready in a few minutes, Mr. Lunghi," Valerie said as she came into the room.

"Huh."

She moved to stand beside him. "Do you like my nature reserve?"

"What reserve?"

"Weren't you admiring my garden? And there's much more in the back."

"More weeds?" the Old Man said. "Someone along the row would help you, I'm sure. Probably you wouldn't have to pay. Just not be so proud you won't ask. And then you could see the view. People would pay for such a view."

"You mean I could sell tickets?" Valerie said. "I'll get the coffee."

The Old Man did not understand what she meant by tickets. Nor did he understand what she meant by a "nature reserve" when he was talking about weeds. He studied the brown, bent stalks near the window. He tried to see some nature. Huh.

"Un rinfresco internazionale," Valerie said as she set a tray on a low table. "The cups are from Verona, where I lived."

196

"With a husband. You said."

"The coffee is from Nicaragua. And the cake is Dundee. I've taken the liberty of cutting you a slice. My mother always made Dundee cakes at Christmas, to have in the house for guests. I try to do the same."

"Christmas?"

"December is upon us." Valerie poured the coffee. "Of course it's not the same kind of holiday in Italy. But even while we were there, I tried to keep the basics of an English Christmas. I felt I owed my daughter that much."

Ah, the daughter. "It's your daughter I want." the Old Man said. "Her address."

"I gave Paula's address to Salvatore last night. Did he lose it?"

"No. It's Salvatore we lost."

"What *will* it take to sort this out, Mr. Lunghi?" Esta said.

"First, keep a record of the nine-nine-nine pages as they occur—time, where you are, and where you've just been."

"Why do you want to know where's she's been?" Northam asked.

"To see whether we can associate some specific activity with when the nine-nine-nine pages are made."

"So according to you we just wait until there have been a hundred calls and then we do a statistical analysis? That's your plan?" Jerry Northam wasn't happy. "And what happens if meanwhile the nutter decides to follow through on them and do something to Esta that means she'll need an ambulance?"

"There's fire and police on nine-nine-nine too, Jerry," Esta said lightly, but the comment only irritated him.

"The only concrete fact we have is that the weekday calls that come are at five past the hour," Angelo said. "That fact doesn't have the significance we first thought, but it does have a significance."

"It signifies that Susan has a mobile," Northam said. "Or has a friend who does."

"If you are suggesting that the calls to the pager are being made in the middle of A-level classes," Angelo said, "you still have to explain why they're always at five past the hour."

Northam scowled but didn't respond. Instead Esta jumped.

"What now?" Northam's increasing irritation was obvious.

"I'm being paged."

Angelo looked at his watch. It read six minutes past eleven.

Esta took the pager from her belt and studied its tiny screen. She closed her eyes and passed the pager to Angelo.

"Six six six?"

"You've got it upside down."

Angelo handed the device back to Esta and wrote the time and day in his notebook. "And where were you before you came here?"

"What? Oh, well, I was at home, and then I left and drove to Bailbrook and picked Jerry up. Then I drove here."

"Was there anybody else in the house when you left?"

"No. Susan would be at school by then and Erik was on his way to the hospital, or so I assume. But no one was in the house."

"What about Mandy?" Northam said.

"Mandy?" Angelo said.

"She cleans and all that. Yes, Mandy was in the house. She's there every morning. But Mandy can't be involved in all this. She wouldn't . . . just doesn't have something nasty like that in her."

Angelo said, "Did you leave your house for any reason this morning before you left for Bailbrook College?"

"Not except to bring in the milk."

"And did you talk to anyone on the telephone? Or see anyone, a neighbor or . . ."

"No."

"And what time did you get to the college?"

"Just past nine-thirty. If we'd left then, we'd have been here on time, but we were delayed." She looked at Northam. "Somebody was playing on his computer."

"Hardly 'playing.' It was an emergency. One of the blip drivers didn't appear for the nine o'clock class and there was nobody else who could fill in."

Esta made a little face but said nothing. Angelo asked, "And where were you during this time?"

"I stood around watching Jerry fly his electronic airplanes."

"You can't expect students to learn how to control air traffic if there's no air traffic to control."

"Whatever," Esta said.

"And when did you leave?"

Northam said, "The class finished at ten, but I stayed to have a word with the AWOL blip driver. Who claimed that he didn't know there was a nine o'clock class."

"Your tone of voice suggests that you don't believe him," Angelo said.

"This particular driver is on his year off before going to

university. He's supposed to have a brain, and knowing the schedule is part of the job." But after a moment Northam said, "I suppose it's possible he was telling the truth. Our class schedules do vary—it's not like we have a class nine to ten every day. And there are always some kids who are better at keeping track than others."

"And after you lectured your blip driver, what did you do?"

"We drove here and came up to your office," Esta said. "Once we found a place to park."

"You're blaming me for that now, are you?" Northam said.

Esta sighed. She turned to Angelo. "Was there anything else, Mr. Lunghi?"

"Yes. I want to page you."

"What?"

"I want to see how long it is from making the telephone call to your receiving your page."

"Why waste even more time?" Northam said. "It's her Susan you ought to be talking to. If she isn't making them herself, she's getting someone to make them. Just tell her if the nine nine nines don't stop, she'll have to go out and make her own living. That'll finish these calls once and for all."

"Shut up, Jerry," Esta said.

"Why should I? It's my money that's being wasted while you shilly-shally because you're worried you might offend that sicko daughter of yours."

"I don't see your sons setting the world on fire. At least mine can read."

Angelo raised his hand, intending to interrupt. But just as he was about to speak, an image of David and Marie bickering came into his mind. Whatever could he to say to these "adults"?

But Angelo's hand proved to be intervention enough. Esta said, "Actually, I've just had a great idea how to stop the nine-nine-nine calls and save your money."

"What?" Northam said.

Esta gave him her pager.

"What's this?"

"No pager, no nine nine nines. No Jerry. End of problem."

"But—"

Esta turned to Angelo. "From our first conversation, I've felt that you're a kind and considerate man, Mr. Lunghi. You don't ever cheat on your wife by any chance, do you? Because anyone married to my husband desperately needs some kindness and consideration in her life. And I sure as hell don't get it from Jerry anymore."

17

*S*alvatore passed the door that led up to the office when he got to Walcot Street. Instead he turned down the next side road and went to the garage where the family's cars were parked. For years they got by on one car, but when Papa managed to buy a second garage space, they soon forgot how they'd ever managed without it.

It was getting on for noon, later than he originally intended to set out for Wellow to interview Paula the Painter. But life with Heather was unpredictable. The woman was at the same time undemanding and totally compelling. She was a different mix of needs and inclinations than any woman he'd been involved with before. And that was no small statement, given the number of women who had passed through Salvatore's life over the years. Angelo once referred to them as Sally's Army.

Both cars were in the garage and Salvatore picked the smaller and newer of them. When he got to Walcot Street, he turned right and headed for Wellsway via Cleveland Bridge. Although it was twice as far as driving through the city center, the longer route would certainly be quicker. Bath traffic was nearly as infamous as its parking problems.

But instead of concentrating on what he wanted to learn from Paula the Painter, Salvatore's thoughts again returned to Heather. What should he do about her? And what did he want to do about her? And what could he do about her?

And even if he decided—like, say, just suppose he did ask her to marry him, which would solve one set of problems—there was no telling what she would answer. He was never sure how she would respond to a suggestion. Yet her flexibilities were good things. His feelings for her were like none he had ever experienced before. But it was not an easy situation. That was the one thing that was certain.

Near the top of the Wellsway hill Salvatore turned left onto the Midford road and passed St. Martin's Hospital. He shook his head and tried to force himself to think about Paula the Painter in Wellow. She had lived with Valerie when Uncle Foxwell still lived next door. So she knew him. And this Paula had a boyfriend, wasn't that what Valerie had said? Jealous of her talent, and what else?

"Will you have some more tea?" Sheila Foxwell asked Gina. "I can add more water."

"No. Thank you."

"Sure?"

Absolutely sure, Gina thought. "I couldn't drink another drop."

"I know what you mean. My bladder has just never been the same since I had this rodent." Sheila Foxwell bounced little Phil on her knee. A fresh gob of snot oozed onto his upper lip.

Gina stood. "I do thank you for talking with me, Mrs. Foxwell."

"When will you get Winston out of jail?"

"I'll do everything I can. But—"

"Yeah, you said. You can't promise." Sheila Foxwell let her shoulders sag. "But I want to ask him about that lottery you said about."

Gina was careful where she stepped as she made her way to the door. "I'll be in touch. Or someone else from my agency will be." Thank you so much, Salvatore, she thought. "And if it is one of the men, you mustn't worry about them. They're all perfectly harmless."

"Will you be seeing my Winston?" Mrs. Foxwell asked as she followed behind.

"I don't really know." Gina opened the door and emerged into the sunlight. She felt like an escapee. "Bye now."

Sheila Foxwell followed as far as the doorway. "If Winston has won the lottery and kept it from me," she called, "tell him I'll swing for him, I really will. Even if it was just a tenner."

Gina walked quickly down the lane. She did not look back. She did not stop. Only when she emerged from High Terrace and turned the corner that was a stone's throw to Lansdown Road and the way home did she slow and take some deep breaths.

And then, ahead of her across the road, she saw the Old Man. He was waiting at a bus stop. Whatever was he doing there?

Gina crossed to him and said, "Fancy seeing you here, Papa."

"I'm on a case."

"What case?"

"Missing person."

"What missing person?"

"You don't think I can find a person who is missing?" the Old Man said.

Oh. Prickly. "You taught us everything we know, Papa, including to make sure your client is paying."

"Of course she pays," the Old Man said. "What else?"

"Well, I've just been to see Mrs. Foxwell, Winston the Murderer's wife. It felt like the longest interview of my life."

"Huh!"

"The woman is daft as a brush with no whiskers. The house is chaotic. She complains constantly, especially about her mother-in-law, and she makes the weakest excuse for tea I've ever tasted. It is a form of torture by dilute milk. And, the wife knows nothing about a lottery win."

After a moment the Old Man said, "I thought this Winston was paying from a lottery."

"That's what he said, and of course money's the solicitor's problem, not ours."

"Huh!"

"I'm on my way back to the office. And you?"

"Me, I have a bus to catch."

When he volunteered no more, Gina said, "Okay, Papa. See you later." She headed off down the hill.

Salvatore missed Paula the Painter's cottage the first time he passed it, although it was on the south edge of the village exactly where Valerie had said it was. But the house was easy to miss because it was obscured by a giant, untrimmed privet hedge.

There wasn't an obvious place for Salvatore to pull in, so he parked at the side of the road and walked back. Passing through a narrow gap in the privet, he saw the stone cottage behind a barrier of dead weeds. Clearly Paula the painter practiced what she preached to her mother.

But although the cottage was small, Salvatore could see that it sat in a considerable amount of land and that at least one outbuilding was in the back.

For a moment he thought about what it might be like to live in such a place. Being outside the city was something he'd never considered, but the right kind of outbuilding would make a good studio.

Suppose he and Heather lived in a place like this. She could have her own business in the house. She could have a child, even more than one. It could run around outside without the constant supervision that would be necessary in a larger place. And that way Heather would always be around to be painted. Hmmm.

On the door there was a wrought-iron knocker in a Celtic shape. Salvatore handled it. Not badly made. Then he knocked. Nothing happened, so he knocked again. When the door opened, he knew immediately that the compact woman before him was Paula the Painter. "You have your mother's eyes," he said.

"No, I don't," Paula said. "I wouldn't blind my own mother."

Paula was smaller than Valerie and had a cherubic face and dark, curly hair that made a good setting for the dazzling blue-black eyes. Salvation said, "I'm sorry to interrupt, but your mother gave me your address."

"Your name is Lunghi, right?"

Salvatore showed surprise. "Yes. Salvatore."

"Mum rang a little while ago. Apparently there's been another of your lot around this morning asking for my address."

"Angelo?"

"She didn't give a name. What's it all about? I mean, I know they dug up Phillip Foxwell's body next door to Mum's, but what's that got to do with me?"

Angelo was closing the computer file of the 999 case when Gina arrived at the office. "Tea," Gina said. "Mainline it. Drip it. Put it on the floor in a bowl, but one way or another I need real tea."

Only when they were on the settee, mugs in hand, did Angelo ask about Gina's visit to Winston Foxwell's wife.

"She's called Sheila and she never met Uncle Phillip Foxwell. But that didn't stop her from talking about how much money he was supposed to have made."

"From building and decorating?" Angelo asked. "Or fencing stolen goods?"

"Not specified. But I'll tell you this, if it is true that Phillip was finicky about his house, he'd have a heart attack if he saw it now. It's chaos. There's dirt everywhere. The child entertains itself by ripping off strips of the wallpaper it's already scribbled with crayons on. It's awful, Angelo. A nightmare." Gina cradled her mug. "Promise me I'll never have to go back there again. Promise."

Rosetta was about to hang up on the assumption that Mama and the Old Man were both out when the telephone was answered and Mama's voice said, "Salvatore?"

"No, Mama. It's Rosetta."

After a pause Mama said, "I thought maybe he found Salvatore." Another pause. "Do you know where Salvatore is, Rose?"

"No, Mama, but if I see him, I'll say you want to talk to him. Okay?"

"Tell him to come to me."

"I'll tell him to come to you," Rosetta said, but she was puzzled. Mama's voice was strange. It was missing its usual energy. Oh, well. Rosetta took a deep breath and prepared to ask what she had called Mama to ask—whether Christopher could formally be offered use of space in the upstairs rooms to teach line dancing now that he had agreed to give teaching a try.

But before Rosetta could start, Mama said, "Thank you, Rose. You're a good girl." And she hung up.

When the bus pulled into the central depot across from the police station, the Old Man got off and made his way to the inquiry window. There he found that the next bus to Wellow left in forty-eight minutes.

Of course Wellow was not so far he couldn't take a taxi. But a bus would save the client money, which was good. She would appreciate.

The Old Man bought a banana from a stall and made his way to the bay from which the Wellow bus would leave. He peeled the banana, dropped the skin in a bin, and then looked for the waiting room. He liked sitting down to eat. Lots of people ate standing, but to him it never appealed.

In the waiting room the Old Man found David. The boy looked pale, not well.

"Granddad?"

"What are you doing here?" Well, waiting for a bus, that was obvious. But a bus to where? Ah, probably back to school, which was up on a hill. "You go to school?"

"I was excused from school. Because I had to go to the dentist."

Which explained the pale. You'd think with all the computers, they'd work out how to make dentists better. "And you're on your way back to school?"

"No. Yes. Sorry. I was confused."

The Old Man held out his banana.

"No thanks, Granddad. I'm not hungry."

Of course he wouldn't want banana. The boy had just come from the dentist.

"Actually, Granddad, I have some time before I have to go back to school."

"You do?"

"Because I finished at the dentist earlier than I thought, so they aren't expecting me back yet. In fact, it's best if I don't go back at all today, because they already gave me all the assignments, and it would only be confusing if I went back, and by the time I got there it would almost be time to leave again for home anyway."

The Old Man didn't follow the full flow of the boy's words. But the gist was that David wasn't going back to school. "I understand."

"So what I wondered is whether you know where Uncle Salvatore is."

"You want Salvatore?"

"Because I haven't seen him in a long time. Well, except

at dinner last night, and he had that woman and I was
with . . ."

The boy seemed to choke on something.

"You're all right?"

"No."

"No?" Well, he'd been to the dentist.

David began to cry. "I'm in love."

"My mother is an extraordinary woman," Paula the Painter
said as she faced Salvatore across the table in her kitchen.

"I couldn't agree more about your mother, although I
only met her yesterday."

"The older I get the more I admire her, not least for the
way she's put up with me."

"She told me about your making her garden into a 'nature
reserve.' Are you a handful otherwise too?"

"Mum let me live in her house for more than five years
after she had every reason to think she'd got rid of me."

"But your father was ill, wasn't he?"

"Yes, along with my ill-conceived marriage, and they both
died, but I lived with Mum for years after that. She even put
up with Simon moving in. We might still be there now if the
two of them got along."

"From what little I know of your mother it's hard for me
to imagine her not getting along with someone."

"It's Simon. He is . . . not easy."

"So you and he moved here?"

Paula counted on her fingers. "Nine years ago. Wow!"

"What does he do?"

"He sculpts in iron. There's a forge out back. We have a
couple of outbuildings."

"And did you both know Phillip Foxwell?"

"In the sense of our being annoying neighbors for each other, yes."

"What was Foxwell like?"

"He struck me as a thoroughly uptight, fussy, bad-tempered little man."

"Come on, don't hold back," Salvatore said lightly. "You can speak freely with me."

But the comment didn't strike Paula as a joke. "All right. I think he was mean-minded, vindictive, petty, malicious, and probably evil. Things had to be exactly the way he wanted them, and to hell with anybody else."

"Oh."

"I got my initiation to Phillip Foxwell when Daddy was ill."

Quietly Salvatore said, "What happened?"

"For the most part we managed to control Daddy's pain, but sometimes it got too much. One afternoon two weeks after I moved back to the house, Daddy screamed. Phillip Foxwell came around to Mum's door and complained. That was how I met him."

"I'm so sorry."

"Especially since he knew full well that Daddy was ill." Paula sighed. Then she chuckled at something that came to mind. "Foxwell *loved* the nature reserve, as you might imagine. At the beginning he just hinted about mowing the grass, but when he realized what we were doing, he went mental. He even went to the Council, to get them to make us cut our 'nasty and invasive weeds.' "

"With what result?"

"The Council pointed out that the restrictions which apply to the Royal Crescent were 'not in force' in High Terrace, that the plants in our garden are all readily available native species. They recommended mediation."

Salvatore laughed.

"Then, mysteriously, areas of the reserve were cut down. It always happened in the middle of the night."

"Urban crop circles?"

"He did it several times."

"You actually saw him?"

"No. But I was so angry that I stood guard sometimes, with a camera. And the fact is that it was those vigils which led me to realize just how wonderful the night is."

"Your mother says you do night paintings."

"I owe it all to Phillip Foxwell. Which, alas, doesn't make me like his memory any better." Paula the Painter sat back. "The idiot just couldn't see the beauty of nature as nature. It's like people who think that you can only be beautiful if you're young. That's such a constricted way of thinking about the world as a whole. My mother's pushing seventy and I think she's more beautiful now than she's ever been. And take flowers. They're great when they're fresh, but they can be fascinating and beautiful at the end of their cycles too. A Phillip Foxwell sees a flower wilt and he thinks, 'Ugh, death.' But to me that denies a whole part of everybody's life and denies its wonderfulness. I adore the shapes and colors that come when a living thing—a flower or whatever—fades and bends and dries."

"So you're looking at the night as a kind of faded day?"

"I've been painting the night for ten years, and sometimes I feel I've only begun to see it. Think of all the daytime paintings there are. There could be just as many of the night."

"Can I see some of your paintings?"

"Are you interested, or just being polite?"

"I'm rarely accused of being polite," Salvatore said. "Truth is, I'm a painter too."

"I thought you were a detective."

"I detect to pay for materials. Speaking of which, did you ever actually see Phillip Foxwell in your garden?"

"No. But Simon did."

"Yeah?"

"Simon saw him come into the garden with a hand scythe."

"What did he do? Simon, I mean?"

"Simon was outside the shed at the foot of Mum's garden—that's where he worked until we moved here. And when Simon wants to work, he doesn't let anything distract him. So, he told me about it the next morning on his way to bed."

"He didn't stop Foxwell?"

"No. But I went next door and confronted the swine. I said we had proof of what he'd been doing and that we would go to the police if another blade of grass or dandelion head or ground-elder leaf was disturbed in the future." Paula laughed. "He slammed the door in my face."

"And when was all this, exactly?"

Paula started counting her fingers. "A long time ago. Years."

"And did he stop?"

"Yes. In fact, I never saw him again."

"I'd like to talk to Simon. Is he here?"

"He's in his studio, but you can't talk to him."

"Why not?"

"He's working."

David blew his nose on his grandfather's cotton handkerchief. He hadn't intended to cry. In fact he hadn't intended to bunk off school at all. But it just got to be . . . too much.

His grandfather said, "So, together we look for Salvatore. Yes?"

Salvatore knew about women. That was the one thing everybody agreed about. Auntie Rose suggested he talk to Salvatore. He would be able to help. David said, "I was going to look for him once I felt a little better. I thought he might be having lunch with that woman."

"Valerie I already tried and Salvatore's not there. But from her I got the address of the daughter in Wellow."

"I don't mean the woman from last night, Granddad. I thought Uncle Sal might be with the other one. The young one."

His grandfather looked surprised. "There's a young one?"

"I saw them in the café at Windows Arts Center. And the people I was with said . . ." But David remembered that among the people he'd been with was Ixy. Oh, Ixy! He snuffled.

"Said what?"

"We all thought the woman and Uncle Sal were together. You know, a couple. They, like, touched each other, and stuff."

"You saw touching? When was this?"

214

"Day before yesterday." David considered. "I went to the dentist that day too." Oh, dear, he thought, if this story ever hits the fan, it's so full of holes it will never fly.

"And your idea was to go there, to this Windows? Is that it?"

David nodded. "I thought I'd go there and wait and see if maybe they came in for lunch, like the other day."

"Well, my idea was to go to Wellow where he should work. But work is not your uncle's favorite. He prefers this painting. So we shall go to your Windows and see what we can see. All right?"

"Call Me Esta is closed?" Gina said.

"Yes," Angelo said.

"So, who made the nine-nine-nine calls?"

"I have no idea. They took us off the case."

"But, why?"

"Because Call Me Esta took the boyfriend off the case too."

"She ditched him?"

"Yes. And already she's looking for a replacement. She asked about my availability."

"To which you replied?"

"I said not if it meant I had to have a pager."

Gina shook her head. She'd only been out of the office a little more than an hour.

"What?" Angelo said.

"How am I going to sleep if I never know who made the nine-nine-nine calls?"

"Sleeping pill?"

"Thanks very much."

"We have no client. Papa would kill us." Angelo spread his hands and mimicked his father's voice: "What way is it to run a business if there's no client who pays?"

"I suppose I could hire you."

"You can't afford me."

"What, there's no discount for sleeping with you?"

"No. That's what I told Call Me Esta too."

But Gina was reminded of something. "What case is Papa on?"

"A case? Papa?"

"I ran into him at a bus stop on Lansdown Road. He said he was on a missing-person case. Who's missing?"

"I don't have the faintest idea."

18

*T*his is your café? A basement?"

"It's part of an arts center, Granddad," David said.

A basement was a basement. And this basement was not far from where Gabriella's Nina wanted her restaurant. If the only competition was a basement, maybe the macaroni-head's idea was better than it seemed.

"Granddad." The boy was tugging his sleeve.

"What?"

"That's her."

"Who?"

"Uncle Sal's friend."

"Where?"

"At the table under the window. She's beautiful, isn't she?"

The Old Man looked toward the table David pointed at. He saw a woman in a loose, rainbow-colored jacket who was sitting with two men. One man was young, with long hair bunched into a tail at the back of his head. The other was older and looked dirty and unshaved. The woman held the older man's hand to her lips. This was Salvatore's young one?

"What do we do now, Granddad?"

For a moment the Old Man watched the woman at the table. She kept the dirty man's hand at her mouth.

"There's no mistake here, David? You're sure this woman was with Salvatore?"

"I know about identification evidence, Granddad. That's her. I'll testify on the witness stand."

At this basement café they ate hands? "Huh!"

"Are you going to talk to her?"

But before the Old Man responded, the three people at the table pushed back their chairs, rose, and walked toward the café door.

The Old Man moved into the woman's path. "Excuse me."

"Can I do something for you?" the woman said. Then she glanced at David. "Oh, hi. You're David, right?"

"Right," David said after a gulp.

She turned back to the Old Man. "So you must be Sal's father."

"I know who I am," the Old Man said. "But who are you?"

"I'm Heather."

"And you are my Salvatore's woman?"

Heather hesitated, but the man with the tail said, "Yep, lock, stock, and barrel."

"Ooo, sore loser," the dirty man said.

"Shut up, both of you." Heather turned to the Old Man. "Salvatore and I are together, Mr. Lunghi, but I'm not 'his' in the possessive sense, and he's not 'mine' either."

"His, mine, I don't know about," the Old Man said. "But I do know my wife worries herself sick about you."

218

"About me?"

"Do you exist, who are you, such things. She worries so much she doesn't eat last night, despite good cooking from Rosetta."

The dirty man said, *"Do* you exist, Heather?"

The tail head said, *"Are* you yourself?"

But Heather waved the two men away. She studied the Old Man's face intently.

"What?" the Old Man said.

"If your wife is unwell," Heather said, "then maybe I can help her. Shall I try? I could come to the house."

When Rosetta found that the office was empty, she slipped through to the kitchen. There Gina was at the table and Angelo stood at the breadboard. "Ah, I thought you might be here," Rosetta said.

"Here is definitely where we are," Angelo said. "I can make you a sandwich? After such a dinner last night it's the least I can do for a sister."

"Thanks." Rosetta slid into a chair next to Gina. "Have you talked to Mama?"

"I was out early doing a Foxwell," Gina said. "But I saw Papa, and he wouldn't be out unless Mama felt better today." Gina frowned. "Would he? Oh, dear. I suppose I should have gone up. The truth is I just forgot, what with one thing and another."

Angelo said, "Papa wouldn't be out if there was anything serious."

"I don't know about that," Rosetta said. "I rang her this morning and she was really strange."

"How?" Angelo said.

"I wanted to talk about Gabriella and the shop premises, but she only talked about Salvatore."

"I thought after Valerie last night she'd be happy," Angelo said. He hummed a few bars of "The Wedding March."

"Hush," Gina said.

"What?" But Angelo turned back to filling Rosetta's sandwich.

"Oh, dear," Gina said, "I really should have gone up."

Rosetta said, "I wondered if maybe what I said about Christopher upset her, him being an undertaker. That's why I haven't brought him home, in case Mama would be upset about what he does."

"Is he the only undertaker?" Angelo said. "Because I got confused when she started asking those other two, Valerie and David's what's-her-name."

"Mama was confused last night," Gina said.

"Christopher's the only undertaker," Rosetta said.

"Right," Angelo said. "Got it."

"As a matter of fact, there is only one female undertaker in the whole Bath-Bristol area."

"So now let me get this completely straight," Angelo said. "You are not dating her, the female one. Am I right?"

"It's not a joke," Rosetta said.

"No. It's a sandwich." Angelo put a plate in front her and sat in his own chair at the table.

"Don't mind your brother," Gina said. "He's a bit manic. Our most beautiful client hit on him this morning, so he says."

"Male or female?"

Angelo doubled up in his chair. "Oooo, I've been touchéd."

The telephone rang. Gina was closest and answered it.

"Maybe it's Mama," Angelo said. "Maybe we should invite her down."

Then Gina said, "What about him?" and Angelo and Rosetta heard concern in her voice. They both turned to watch her and listen.

Mama was sitting in her chair by the window when she heard the tap on the door. It was a light tap, almost hesitant. If the television had been on, she wouldn't have heard it. If the washing machine had been on, she wouldn't have heard it. But nothing was on. No television, no washer, no Salvatore. She turned back to the view from the window. Being so high and facing the river, it was beautiful. Even in December.

The tap repeated and Mama looked toward the door. This tapper was definitely not Salvatore. His knock was robust, manly. And Salvatore would try if the door would open before he knocked a second time.

When the tap came again, Mama rose and answered it. Outside on the landing was a young woman. She was a round-faced girl but in a nice-looking way, a Madonna-ish way. Madonna the mother of Jesus, not Madonna the girl singer.

"Mrs. Lunghi?" the Madonna-faced woman said.

"Yes."

"I'm Heather."

"Who?"

"Hasn't your husband spoken to you about me?"

221

Mama tried to remember if the Old Man had spoken about a Heather. She didn't remember one, but to be truthful, today she might not remember. She wasn't feeling very good.

Heather said, "Maybe he hasn't had a chance to ring you yet. We agreed that I would come over later this afternoon, and he gave me a key to the door downstairs because he was so sure you'd want to see me. But I've just learned that I have to go someplace with some business colleagues later. I don't have your phone number or I would have rung. So, instead of missing you altogether I came over hoping he'd already rung you. I understand that you're not feeling well. I think I might be able to help."

"You are Heather?"

"Yes. I'm Salvatore's girlfriend."

Mama peered harder at the girl. "But you don't look like an undertaker."

"I'm not."

"Oh." A girlfriend? And not an undertaker. "You're sure you're Salvatore's girlfriend?"

"Not so much a girl these days, and not Salvatore's in the possessive sense, but, yes, Mrs. Lunghi. Your Sal and I are together. We've been together for about three months."

"Together?"

"A couple. Dating. Seeing each other." Heather waved her hands. "You know, good times."

"And this is for three months, you say?" Mama felt the number register. This woman was saying that she had been Salvatore's woman for all the time he wasn't bringing women to dinner.

"Well, let's see. If we're counting properly, it's a little longer than that. We met at the end of August."

"The end of August?" Mama said. "So long?"

"It adds up," Heather said with a smile.

The Madonna-woman had a nice smile. But three months? Or this more? And never did Salvatore bring this woman of three months to dinner? "But why? What's wrong with you?"

Instead of answering, Heather said, "Today, Mrs. Lunghi, isn't the question what's wrong with you?"

As soon as Gina hung up the telephone, Angelo asked, "What's wrong?"

"It was the school secretary, about David."

"What's happened?" Angelo and Rosetta spoke the same words.

"I don't know." Gina looked up and saw the concerned looks on the two faces. "Oh, it's not an accident or anything. He's not injured."

"So what did they say?" Angelo said.

"She asked me if it wasn't possible to reschedule his dental treatments."

"What?"

"The woman asked if we couldn't make David's dental appointments for of-out-school hours. She said that most dentists understand, and when the treatments are extensive and ongoing, they'll organize appointments so that the child doesn't have to miss classes."

"David's teeth?" Angelo said.

"I didn't know David was having dental work," Rosetta said.

"Neither did I," Gina said.

. . .

After the taxi drove slowly through the village, the driver stopped beside some tall, dense hedges and said, "That must be it."

"These are privet?" David's grandfather seemed uncertain.

"As privet as the day is long," the driver said.

"What?"

"As privet as the driven snow, sir."

"He's sure, Granddad," David said.

"So why doesn't he say?" But the Old Man opened the door and got out. To the driver he said, "You can wait here?"

"It's your nickel, mate."

"Nickel? What nickel?"

"It's what the Yanks say," the driver said. "Me and the missus was over there last month and it's a cracking place. I loved every minute."

The Old Man turned to David and said, "Is he mad, this taxi? Do you understand?"

"He's happy to wait, Granddad."

"So why talk about nickel? Are we mining engineers?"

David said to the driver, "We won't be long. We're pretty sure my uncle is here."

"Top hole, old bean," the driver said.

David saw his grandfather register "bean," so he took the Old Man's elbow and led him through the gap in the hedge. "Knock on the door, Granddad. See if this Paula is here."

"Nickel, huh!" the Old Man said, but he banged with the knocker. The cottage door opened almost immediately. "You are Paula the Painter?"

"Yes. And you are—"

"I know who I am, but I have a taxi talking beans. I want to see to my Salvatore."

"He's not here, Mr. Lunghi."

"You're sure? Because he left this Heather to come here, for the Foxwell."

"He was here a while ago, and we talked about Phillip Foxwell. But I told him what I knew and he left."

"Granddad."

"How long ago was this leaving?" the Old Man asked.

"Maybe half an hour ago. Or maybe a bit more. I don't have a watch, but I'd guess it was about that."

"No watch?" the Old Man said.

"Granddad." David tugged on his grandfather's sleeve.

"I listen to Radio Four," Paula said. "I can tell the time by what's on."

"Granddad."

"What, David?"

"If Uncle Sal left half an hour ago, how come one of our cars is parked out there on the lane?"

"I'm not an undertaker, Mrs. Lunghi," Heather said. "I'm a saliva therapist."

"You're a what?" Mama said.

"A saliva therapist."

Mama considered the words. She had never heard of such a thing. "You mean spit?"

"It's an ancient art, Mrs. Lunghi. Two thousand years ago the Greeks used snake saliva to help the healing of wounds."

"Greeks did?" Mama shook her head. She had invited

225

this woman into her house, but now instead of Salvatore the woman talked of snake healing and Greeks. It was confusing.

"Everybody knows about licking your wounds," Heather said, "but, believe me, there is a world more healing in saliva than just that."

"By *saliva,* you mean exactly what?"

"Well, there are three major gland pairs in the mouth, and lots of minor glands."

"Oh."

"And they're located in many different parts of the mouthplace."

Mama stared at Heather's Madonna-eyes.

"Of course each gland makes its own special contribution to the mixture we know as whole saliva, but for most purposes those of us who practice as saliva therapists utilize the growth factors secreted by the major gland pairs."

"Oh."

"But even taking only the three major glands and ignoring the minor salivas, there are still lots of different proportions you can mix. Which you use depends entirely on the problem you want to treat."

"By treat . . ." A doctoring image was hard to fit with this nice-looking, well-spoken, round, young woman in her coat of many colors.

"Yes?"

"By treatment with this saliva, you mean you lick?"

"That's one thing I do," Heather said, "if it's indicated. But more often I use the patient's own saliva and apply it with one of my saliva brushes." She patted her bag. "Although for other conditions a saliva dip is best."

"You collect spit?"

"There's is a range of collection techniques. For instance, if you just think of a lemon—"

"A lemon?"

"Think of a slice of lemon in your mouth."

Mama thought.

"Now, doesn't it feel wet under your tongue?"

It did. But wasn't it always wet under a tongue?

"That's where the submandibular gland is."

"Heavens."

"For other glands we have special collection cups. For instance, I'm one of the first therapists in this country with a pair of Swedish SLURP cups." From her bag Heather withdrew two small, curved pieces of plastic.

"A pair, oh my."

"They're a symmetrical because you need a right-handed one and a left-handed one. We use them to collect pure parotid secretions."

"Tell me something. Does my Salvatore know about these glands and slurps, these lickings and dips?"

The Old Man followed David and Paula the Painter into the lane through the gap in the hedge. The taxi driver started his engine, but the Old Man shook his head. "More nickel."

David pointed and said, "That's one of ours, isn't it, Granddad?"

The car, which was small and blue like the Aegean in the afternoon, certainly looked like one of the Lunghi cars. "Look inside," the Old Man said.

David dashed ahead. "Nobody," he called. "But it is ours." He recited the registration number.

"Is it your car, Mr. Lunghi?" Paula asked.

"David knows."

"Are you sure?"

"Of course I am sure." The Old Man faced the young woman. "What have you done with my Salvatore?"

"I . . . I . . ."

"Well?"

"He said he was leaving."

"First 'he left.' Now 'he said he was leaving.' Not the same."

The Old Man saw Paula look at the area behind her cottage. "I suppose it's possible that he tried to talk to Simon."

"So show me this Simon," the Old Man said.

Paula crossed the road and slipped through a narrow space between the end of the privet hedge and the fence that bounded the neighboring field.

The Old Man followed, and David followed him.

Once she was on the other side of the gap, Paula broke into a trot.

Both Lunghis did too.

19

With nothing to be done about David until he got back from wherever he was that wasn't school, Gina and Angelo tried to turn their attentions to working out what work needed to be done in the afternoon.

But no sooner had Angelo scribbled out the information for Rosetta to prepare the 999 case invoice than the telephone rang.

Gina was not closest to the phone but she was quickest. "Gina Lunghi."

Angelo and Rosetta watched her closely.

"Yes," Gina said to the caller.

Angelo tried to work out the meaning of her neutral tone, whether her control was real or pretend. He did not have long to wait to find out. Gina said, "Why not?" and then hung up. She turned to him. "Your girlfriend."

"My what?"

"Call Me Esta. She's in a call box around the corner and she wants to see us as soon as possible."

"Why?"

"I didn't ask. Maybe to give you your pager."

"But—"

"I'm going to Mama's. You coming, Rose?"

"Yes," Rosetta said, and before Angelo knew it, they were gone. There was nothing left for him to do but go through to the office. And when he got there, Esta was already at the downstairs door.

"I just couldn't leave things unresolved like that, Mr. Lunghi," Esta said when she entered the office.

Angelo was about to ask if she would like some tea, but then he decided not to. He wasn't feeling sympathetic to Call Me Esta. And to offer tea was more than just to offer tea. Tea was a gift.

"First I want to apologize about what happened this morning."

But so much had happened in their meeting that, when Esta did not immediately amplify her comment, Angelo asked, "What is it you're apologizing for?"

"Jerry and I were terribly rude."

Yes, he supposed they were. But he had witnessed worse. "Not to worry."

"It's unforgivably bad manners to squabble before strangers. And it's worse to inflict a private moment like breaking up."

"So, you are still broken?"

"Oh, yes. I never look back in relationships."

Only in rearview mirrors? "And is that it, what you wanted?"

"No. I need to know how much it would cost for me to hire you."

"Hire us?"

"Yes." Esta smiled, and with the smile, her radiance returned. "Is there any discount for repeat customers?"

Discounts. Hmmm. "Would you like a cup of tea?" Angelo said.

Usually when Gina knocked, Mama would call out, "It's open." But no call came this time, so Gina tried the handle. The door was unlocked. Gina glanced at Rosetta, opened the door, and stepped in.

At first Gina did not recognize what she saw. Mama was sitting in her favorite chair, but an unfamiliar woman was balancing herself on the chair's arm. The woman seemed to be using a brush to paint Mama's forehead. Although Mama's eyes were closed, one of her cheeks appeared swollen.

"Mama? Are you all right?" Gina moved into the room. "What's going on?"

Behind Gina, Rosetta said, "Mama?"

But without opening her eyes, Mama said, "Shit down, girls. We won't be long."

Gina was dumbfounded. Mama spoke as if something was in her mouth, but she looked serene. And the strange woman did not acknowledge the newcomers at all.

"Shit," Mama said again.

Gina said, "We're sorry to disturb you, Mama. We'll wait for you downstairs, won't we, Rose?"

"We will," Rosetta said. The two women backed out of the room.

"So," Angelo said as the kettle boiled, "what do you want to hire us for?" He wondered if he should make a joke about whether it was just him as a boyfriend she wanted to hire, or whether there would be other functions as well. He decided not to.

"It's the nine nine nines."

"The same nine nine nines?" Angelo said lightly. "Or are there new ones?"

"The same." But Esta's voice was suddenly so faint that Angelo turned from the kettle to see if his client was all right. She perched on the edge of the settee and looked smaller and more fragile than Angelo remembered her. This client was a chameleon client. He was sorry that he had been flippant.

"The tea's ready soon. What about the nine nine nines?"

"I don't have the damned pager anymore, but the person who made those awful calls is still out there. And I don't know what it all means."

Esta looked so sad that Angelo felt an impulse to comfort her. To pat her head, to put a reassuring arm around her shoulders, to say it would be all right. Why such an urge? he wondered. Esta was not urging.

He turned to the boiling water and filled the teapot. He stirred the leaves. Was it a good thing to comfort a client with an arm on the shoulders? Or was it a bad thing, sending wrong signals, like the 999s themselves?

Perhaps the truth was that he feared that Esta's jokes about his taking Pager Jerry's place might not be jokes at all. Perhaps he feared that she would respond to such comfort by falling into his arms saying, "Thank you, Angelo. I feel so much better."

He poured the tea and took her a mug. Or instead was his fear a wishful one?

"Thank you, Angelo." When she smiled, she was without question a beautiful woman. But he was no Salvatore. Besides, with his luck, no sooner would he comfort Esta than Gina would walk in.

"You're welcome," Angelo said.

Then Gina walked in.

"I feel so much better," Mama said as Heather dried her SLURP cups and packed them in her bag. "Thank you."

"I'm pleased if I've helped." Heather passed Mama a small bottle. "If you keep it in the fridge, it will stay active for at least a week." Heather gave Mama a small brush. "Paint the skin at the hairline on your forehead and where your ears connect to your head if you begin to feel tense again."

"I would never have expected to feel good from such a thing."

Heather smiled. "Actually I hear that a lot."

"And do you make a living from this saliva?"

"Not yet. I only finished my training in the summer. But I'm getting together a group of people who each have a different specialist therapy. We're going to open a treatment center together."

"Ah, I think perhaps I have seen such places. They are alternating, yes?"

"There are centers already for so-called alternative therapies," Heather said. "But most of the treatments they offer are so common now that they're really establishment treatments all over again, don't you think?"

"Oh."

"My friends and I want to offer genuinely alternative therapies. You could call us alternative alternative."

"I could?"

"That's what you'll get at our center." Heather smiled. "At least you will once we find ourselves suitable premises."

"Premises? You look for premises?"

"That's why I couldn't come later. I'm sure your husband intended to tell you about me before I arrived. If I'd known you weren't expecting me, I don't think I'd have just arrived saying, 'Hi'—big smile—'I'm Heather, Sal's saliva-therapist girlfriend.' Will you explain to your husband for me?"

"I will explain."

"One of my friends found an empty shop that might be perfect. But the only time we can see it today is later this afternoon, so . . ."

"Well, if it's not so perfect," Mama said, "let me know. It's possible that I might be able to help you. Who knows?"

"Really?"

"And to think, you are my Salvatore's woman for three months." Mama smiled.

"Yes. Although not 'his' in the possessive sense."

"Not possessive. That I must remember. And to think, in all that time, not once did my Salvatore—" But Mama interrupted herself. "For me, 'my' Salvatore is possessive, because he is mine. But that doesn't mean I won't share. You understand?"

"Of course, Mrs. Lunghi."

"And Mama, call me Mama. In whatever sense. Will you do that?"

"Of course I will, Mama."

"I was saying, to think that in all those three months . . . Or was it maybe more than three?"

"A little more than three months, yes."

"But not four?"

"Not four. Three months and about a week."

"Ah, she counts. This is so sweet. So romantic. And to think, in all the time of months and a week not once does my Salvatore bring you here to meet me."

"To be frank with you, Mama, I think that Sal's a little sensitive about what I do." She shook her treatment bag.

Mama shook her head. "No."

"No?"

"That's not why he did not bring you to dinner. Not your saliva."

"You don't think so?"

"Me, I think what Salvatore was shy about bringing to dinner was a girlfriend who is pregnant."

Heather blinked. "But . . . how . . . ? How did you know?"

"How did I know? I look at you. I see you move. I listen. Of course I would know. A mother knows about such things."

They found Salvatore in a crumpled pile in front of an outbuilding behind Paula the Painter's cottage.

From a distance it looked as if he might be napping against the wall by the door. But his position was awkward for sleep. And the side of his head was red.

"Uncle Sal!" David sprinted from behind his grandfather to beat both the adults to where Salvatore's body lay.

A moment later Paula was crouched in the grass with her hands together over her nose and mouth. "Oh no, oh no, oh no, oh no," she wailed.

The Old Man knelt by his son. He felt the boy's neck for a pulse.

"Is he all right, Granddad?"

"David," the Old Man said calmly, "go to the taxi."

"I want to stay here."

"Go to the taxi, David. Tell the nickel to call an ambulance on nine nine nine. Tell him to explain to the ambulance how to find us."

"Yes, Granddad."

"Run, David. You run."

David ran to the road.

"Oh no, oh no, oh no."

"And you, Paula," the Old Man said.

"Oh no, oh no."

The crouching position was difficult for the Old Man to get out of. He used the wall to help himself up. He walked to where Paula the Painter was oh-no-ing. He tapped her head. "Stop the noise."

But she didn't stop, so he tipped her face up by the chin. "You, Paula. Go in your house. Bring me blankets out here so that I can warm my bleeding son. Do you hear what I say?"

Paula pushed his hand away and stood.

"Blankets, now. Do you hear me?"

Paula ran for the house.

The Old Man turned back to Salvatore. He took his jacket off and then knelt again, to wrap it around the boy. But as he did, the door to the outbuilding opened.

"I've been thinking about your nine nine nines," Gina said to Esta as Angelo poured more tea.

"Did your angel of a husband explain what happened this morning?"

236

"Yes," Gina said with a glance at Angelo. "But I can understand why you don't want to leave it unresolved."

Angelo brought the tea. "Have a biscuit," he said. Esta took a biscuit.

Gina said, "Esta, what I want to do next is talk to your daughter."

"Susan? Why?"

"Because it was your feeling that she was involved."

"But you said—"

"She didn't make the calls, but I think we were too quick to ignore your instinct about her. I think we should have done more to follow up on your gut feeling."

"If there might be some point then, by all means, talk with Susan."

"Thank you," Gina said. "I'll go to her school today."

"But," Esta said, "what if she doesn't know anything?"

"Then we're probably dealing with a madman," Gina said lightly.

"What the fuck is it now?" the man who loomed above the Old Man said. He was dark and stocky. The Old Man saw that his bloodshot eyes gleamed with anger.

"Good you should come out." The Old Man found the wall with his hand and struggled to his feet. He saw that the angry man held a pair of tongs. "I was going to knock."

"What is the matter with you people?" the angry man screamed. "I say to go away. But you keep coming, and you won't shut the fuck up. I must be left alone. I must have quiet. Don't you people understand English?"

"English?" the Old Man said, his voice rising. "English?

This is English, what you did to my boy?" He took a step forward.

The angry man raised his tongs. "Stop."

"This is English, with your metal tool against his poor painter's head?"

"Stay where you are." The angry man's voice was furious. But he moved backward.

With two more steps the Old Man's nose was all but touching the angry man's face. "This is English?" The Old Man grabbed a handful of hair and bent the angry man over Salvatore. "This is what you call English?"

For a moment the angry man was still. "Is he . . . ?"

"This is my son. My son."

But the angry man came alive again and twisted away. He shouted, "He got what he deserved. First he goes to Paula's studio. Then he knocks here to brag about it. If he's dead, bury him yourself. I won't help you. I've got work to do."

20

When Esta's daughter, Susan, was shown into the deputy head's office, she struck Gina as about the most unlikely daughter imaginable for Esta Dumphy. It was not just that her hair was dark—nearly black—where Esta's was fair. Nor that she was pale and tiny. But the girl's face was so flat and undefined it almost looked as if it had been pressed against a board. The only positive feature was her eyes, which were dark brown and intense.

"They say I have to see you," Susan said. "Do I know you? I don't, do I? What's going on?"

"Susan, I am a private detective working on a serious case, and I need to ask you a few questions."

"A private detective? Is someone dead?"

Susan's direct stare caught Gina off guard as much as the direct question did. "No. Why? Are you expecting someone to be dead?"

Susan shook her head, so vigorously that Gina was reminded of a dog shaking off water. "Nooooo," Susan said in a whiny way. "But there's always something to screw me up at important times."

"Important times? Do you mean Christmas?"

"Don't be an ass."

"How is this an important time, Susan?"

"The prize. I'm receiving a prize for a project I did. There's a dinner next week. Princess Anne and all that. It's not cool to care, but I do." She shrugged.

"And when good things happen to you something usually screws them up?"

"Yeah. But that's not your business. It's family stuff."

"My 'business' does involve family stuff, of a kind."

"What?"

"Your mother has been getting threatening messages on her pager." When Susan said nothing, Gina said, "Do you know what a pager is?"

Susan nodded slowly. Her eyes fixed on Gina and she was so motionless and intent that it felt like a challenge.

Gina stared back. Her eyes began to hurt, but she refused to blink.

Susan said, "So, it's true."

"What's true?"

"Mum's having an affair. Louis said she was, but I didn't believe him."

Angelo was in the kitchen when Marie came home from school. Before either decided to greet the other, the telephone rang. Marie was standing closer, but she did not answer it.

Angelo and Marie looked at each other as three rings became four. "Marie?"

"I'm not allowed to talk on the telephone." She whirled around and left the kitchen.

By the time Angelo picked up the phone and said, "Hello?" the answering machine message had begun. "I am here," he shouted. "Angelo Lunghi. The message will finish in a few seconds."

But when the message did finish, there was a pause at the other end of the line.

"Hello? Who is it?"

A young female voice said, "Is, uh, is David there?"

"David? No, he isn't here. Do *you* know where he might be?"

"I thought he might be there. I'll try later, maybe."

"Who is this?"

"No, no message." And the young woman hung up.

Angelo stood, phone in hand. He knew that he had heard the voice before. Was it that Ixy? Most likely it was. Unless . . . Unless it was Marie's Cassie! Only asking for David because she knew Marie would not be allowed to talk.

The notion was irritating. So Angelo dialed 1471 to get the number of the caller. A BT recorded voice said, "You were called today at sixteen twenty-three hours. The caller withheld their number."

That irritated Angelo even more. It wasn't that the possibly devious young woman had anticipated a 1471 and had dialed 141 to conceal her number. What irritated Angelo was the message. "The" caller, "their" number. Such grammar? Huh!

Gina parked in one of the visitors' spots at Bailbrook College. She looked at the steps of the old manor house that was the college administration building. She did not want to run into Jerry Northam if she could help it.

But Northam was not in evidence. So she got out and turned toward the much newer brick building where the teaching of air traffic control took place.

Just inside the main entrance she found a dozen or so people. They were of varied ages, although many were young. Nearly half were female, and Gina asked one of the women for directions.

"Ze bleeps?" the woman said. "I am not knowing how . . ." Then she spoke to another of the women in a language that to Gina sounded a bit like French but wasn't.

The second woman took Gina's arm and led her to a double door. "You mus' down thees cordoor, on left turn. Then right."

"Thank you." Gina headed through the doors, resolved to ask again.

At the end of the corridor Gina paused. The closed doors on the left and the right had no markings to help her decide which way to go. But then one of the doors opened. A pimply, pear-shaped young man nearly ran her down.

"Uh, sorry," he grunted.

The young man had an anorak on and looked exactly the way Gina expected a blip driver to look. "Are you Louis?"

"Uh, no. He's inside." The pear gestured to the door he'd just barged through. "Uh, I got to catch the bus." And although there was plenty of room in the corridor, he clipped Gina's shoulder with his own as he passed her. "Uh, sorry."

Marie was in her room, heels on the windowsill. She was home from school, sure, but there was nothing to do. She sighed and stared at the clouds in the sky. She had no future.

Listlessly, she stretched an arm to the floor and retrieved her bag. From it she took a cigarette. She rolled it between her fingers. She sniffed the tobacco. She sniffed the filter.

She didn't particularly feel like smoking the thing, but what else was there to pass the time with? Her mother would tell her to get on with her homework. Her father would say to clean her room. Or maybe the other way around. But those were the last things she would do now, after all the kerfuffle. After they acted as if they didn't believe her. She sighed again.

At this time on a normal day she would either be with Cassie or talking to her on the telephone. They would be reviewing what had happened at school. But it was not a normal day. There might never be a normal day again.

Marie fished in her bag for a lighter. If she opened the window and leaned out, she could smoke the cigarette, probably even get away with it if someone came in. Maybe it would be a good idea to burn a bit of paper inside the room first. Then, if asked, she could say the smell was the paper. That's what they did at Cassie's when Cassie wanted a fag. Although Cassie's mother almost never came into Cassie's room. Cassie's mother was cool.

Marie stood up, putting the cigarette and lighter on the seat of her chair. She was just about to open her window when there was a tap on her door. She froze. Her father walked in.

"What do *you* want?" Marie said, turning to him.

Her father seemed surprised by the sharpness of her tone, but he didn't leave. "I know it's not the best time. I know we're in the middle of some problems."

"I don't have any problems," Marie said. "You're the ones with problems."

"I don't want to talk about all that."

"Neither do I. Not until you have something sensible to say." The comment came out of her mouth more quickly than she expected. It made her sound like a parent talking to a child. Cassie was going to love hearing about it. She'd say, "You never!" and Marie would say, "Oh yes I did." If she ever got to talk to Cassie again.

"It's about David," Angelo said.

David? "What about David?"

"We got a call from the school. They say he's been leaving to go to dentist's appointments."

"Is something wrong with his teeth?"

"He had a checkup last week. But he told the school that he had another appointment."

It broke upon Marie that David was in trouble. The smarty-aleck little goody-goody was actually in trouble. And if David was in trouble, people wouldn't get on her case so much. There might be life after idiot George Skillman after all. Yes! "You mean he's been bunking off classes by saying it's to go to the dentist?"

"It very much looks that way. He's done it at least twice this week, including today."

Twice in a week? No, no. Trust child David to take a perfectly good skive and overplay it. "So what's the brainless brain been doing?"

"I don't know. That's what I wanted to ask. Do you have any idea where he might be now?"

"None, Pa."

"Because we're worried about him."

"Don't worry about David. Don't waste your time. You know that whatever he's been doing, it must have been boring and nerdy and otherworldy." But the comment didn't seem to reassure her father.

"I wondered about that girl."

"What about her?"

"Well . . ."

David cutting school with Ixy? To snog her, or to . . . The thought was too repellent to contemplate. Besides, it couldn't be true. "Ixy was in school this afternoon, Pa. I saw her in Drama. In fact she asked me where David was."

"Oh."

"But you could call her house. Maybe she found him. I know she's keen."

"But if she was at school . . ."

"The only thing I do know, Pa, is that when he shows up, he's bound to have some wild, absurd tale to tell."

"He will?"

"That's how extraterrestrials try to cover their tracks."

Inside the pear-shape's door, Gina discovered tables with large television-like boxes on them. But there were no people.

Then she heard voices from nearby. She found the speakers in a second, narrower room. This too had television-like screens but in pairs, one above the other in four positions. Along with each pair of screens were a computer keyboard, a mouse, and a grid of illuminated buttons.

A woman of about thirty sat at the end of the room. She wore a light blue sweater, jeans, and headphones. Standing behind her was a boy dressed in black who looked hardly older than David. He wore headphones too, but he turned as Gina came in and said, "Yes?" with an air of authority.

"Are you Louis?"

He said, "Advance to level two," then turned back to the woman. "Remember the wind speed, Mrs. Portway."

Gina said, "Louis, I need to speak with you."

Louis glanced at Gina. "Can't it wait?"

"No."

"Well, what is it about?"

"Susan gave me your name."

"Oh, yeah?"

"Yeah."

"Mrs. Portway," Louis said, "are you all right on your own for a minute?"

"I think so."

"Just don't crash anything, okay? I hate the sight of blood."

Mrs. Portway chuckled nervously as Louis pushed a clump of hair off his forehead and took a few steps toward Gina. "We'll be next door." Louis led Gina to the room she'd just passed through.

As he pulled out two chairs, he picked up one of numerous small plastic racks on the tables in front of the television-like screens. "This is where we teach controlling traffic manually. They still need it for small airports."

"I'm not interested in airports."

"Neither is Suze. She likes bugs. Real ones, I mean. Not computer glitches. But me, I think air traffic control systems are wowsome. I may well come back after uni. They've got a whole building here where they design control systems to fit individual airport topographies and traffic patterns. What they do down there has been eye-opening. If you can do the maths." Louis wrinkled his nose. "Which Suze can't. Will this take long? What did Suze give you my name for?"

"So we could talk about the nine-nine-nine pager messages you've been leaving."

Louis looked at Gina blankly.

"We thought my coming here would be better than sending the police."

"The police?" Louis looked puzzled.

For just an instant it crossed Gina's mind that she was wrong. Could this boy genius, who wanted to impress Esta's Susan so badly that he inundated her with presents and puzzles and invitations, in fact be innocent of the 999 harassment?

But then Louis covered his mouth and giggled. "All I did was warn Mrs. Dumphy. What's wrong with that?"

"Warn her about what?" Gina asked, emphasizing each word.

"She's shagging old Northam."

"What on earth makes you think that?"

Louis stared. "Come on, of course she is. She's out here with him all the time. Nine nine nine, fire, it might get too hot to handle. Nine-nine-nine police, you might get caught. Nine-nine-nine ambulance, could be dangerous. And old Northam has a reputation. He hits on the female students. He's been through about a dozen since I've been here."

Gina waited.

Louis giggled nervously again. "I thought warning Mrs. D. about him before it broke up the marriage would make Suze happy."

. . .

Mama came into the kitchen looking for someone to talk to, but she found it empty. "Angelo?" she called. "Gina? Rose?"

Her calls produced Marie. "Hi, Grandma."

"No one is here?"

"Dad's the only one I've seen lately. Maybe he's in the office."

"Ah, the office."

"I don't know where Mum or Auntie Rose are. David is on another planet."

"A planet? Goodness."

"It's such a shame he's gone to the bad, isn't it?" Marie said. "If he used his talents more wisely, he could be such a nice, responsible boy."

"In your list you don't mention your grandfather. Do you know where he is? Because I want to save some money."

"I haven't seen him either. Maybe he's out looking for David."

"It's Salvatore he looks for." Mama dug in her purse. "I want you to have this." She gave Marie a ten-pound note.

"Wow. Thanks, Grandma."

"And I have one for David too, when he gets back from his planet."

"I'll give it to him for you, if you like."

"You're such a good girl, Marie." Mama passed over a second note.

"Thanks again," Marie said. "But, what's it for?"

"For it being a good day. I feel so much pressure lifted. I feel ten years stronger."

"So, a pound a year?"

"And why not? My Salvatore is all right."

"Grandma, could I be cheeky and ask you another favor? Could I use the telephone in your flat to make a call? I won't be long."

"Just don't make a nine nine nine," Mama said happily.

Angelo was on the telephone in the office. "And if those girls come back to the shop, Mrs. Corman, just let me know. Okay?"

As he listened to what Mrs. Corman said in response, Angelo winked at Rosetta, who sat on the settee. He gave a thumbs-up. Rosetta applauded silently. And after a few more minutes Angelo completed the call and hung up. "Good idea, Sis. But now, will Marie agree?"

"Why wouldn't she?"

"Search me, but I have no way of telling what that girl will or won't do these days."

They both heard the street door fly open and bang against the wall. They heard feet running up the stairs. "Who can that be?" Rosetta asked.

"Well, Watson," Angelo said, "my deductive powers tell me it's somebody under seventy years of age. Furthermore, unless I miss my mark, he has perfect teeth and a cover story."

A moment later David ran into the room. Breathlessly he said, "Dad, Auntie Rose . . . It's Uncle Sal . . ." David bent over, gasping.

Angelo winked again at Rosetta. "What's that about Uncle Sal?"

"Granddad . . . found him . . ."

"That's good," Rosetta said, "because Mama thought he was lost."

"No . . ." David raised a hand.

"Yes," Angelo said, "and he wasn't the only one who was lost. Tell me, David Lunghi, just what do you think you're doing telling the school you had dental appointments when you had nothing of the kind?"

"Dad . . ."

"Did you really think that we weren't going to find out? For a clever boy you can be pretty dim sometimes."

"Dad!"

Angelo heard more footsteps on the stairs. At the same time, Marie came into the office from the house. "Look, it's Davy! Surprise, surprise. I heard your clippety-cloppy bang-bang-bang all the way from my room, Dippy Dental Dave. So were you been? Aliens kidnapped you because they're starting their own wonk breeding program?"

David said, "Dad! A man hit Uncle Sal on the head."

Angelo frowned. It was not a very nice concoction.

"I saw our car," David said. "And then Granddad stood up to the man and sent him back in his room."

"What car?" Rosetta asked. "What man?"

"They get incoherent when they lie," Marie said.

Gina came into the office. "Somebody left the outside door open. Oh, David, there you are. Where on earth have you been?"

"Not on earth, Mum," Marie said.

"And whatever do you think you're up to telling the school you had fictitious dental appointments? Do you have any idea how worried we were?"

"Sorry, Mum, but—"

As Mama entered the office, she said, "There you are,

everybody. It's good you're together, because I have things to tell."

David put his hands on his forehead and shouted, "Stop! Stop! Stop! Granddad sent me to tell you all something."

"So tell," Mama said. "I've waited so many months, I can wait a few minutes more."

21

*T*he Old Man sat by Salvatore's bed. The boy's eyes were closed. "Salvatore? Are you there?"

"Yes, Papa."

"How do you feel?"

"About the same as thirty seconds ago."

"You're counting? A good sign."

"We don't need signs. I'm all right."

"You I don't believe. The doctors I believe."

"What do the doctors say?" Salvatore shifted slightly, turned toward his father, and opened his eyes.

"They say that you should stay awake until they develop the pictures of your head."

"I'm sure they won't find anything."

"I agree. Hollow."

"I meant . . ." Then Salvatore understood. "On my death-bed and you make jokes."

"You made the joke."

After a moment Salvatore said, "Yeah, I did, didn't I?"

The Old Man took his son's hand and squeezed.

Salvatore squeezed back. "You saved my life maybe?"

"Maybe. But maybe your head is so hard the wrought iron bounces off."

"Bonces off?"

"Jokes, jokes, jokes."

Salvatore took a deep breath. "Did he tell you why he hit me, Papa?"

"For knocking, he said to me. To the police he will think up something better."

"I did knock on his door. When he didn't answer, I knocked again. It disturbed him."

"For such a thing he hits, maybe kills? Is he crazy?"

"He's an artist, Papa. For artists, creative times mustn't be disturbed." After a pause Salvatore said, "That was meant to be a joke, Papa. Not very good, huh?"

"Maybe yes and maybe no. But something I want to say to you."

"What?"

"About my son the painter, if painter is what he wants." When Salvatore said nothing, the Old Man said, "You hear me?"

"Yes, Papa."

"A man with wrought iron is in front of you, and you don't step back? Maybe for you detective is too dangerous. So, be a painter. With my blessing."

After a moment, Salvatore said, "Really?"

"Paint my picture. Is that really enough?"

"I'd like that." Then, "You have a very interesting head."

"My head is interesting?"

"Yeah. I've always wanted to paint it."

"What color?"

"Blue."

The Old Man chuckled. "We make a joke."

A nurse came into the room. "Mr. Lunghi?"

Salvatore and the Old Man said, "Yes?" in unison. They both laughed.

The nurse said, "I'm glad you guys are having a good time, but there are six people in the waiting room who seem pretty upset."

Mama saw the Old Man first. She ran to him in the corridor. "My Salvatore, he's all right? What's wrong? I want to see. Where is he? He's all right?"

"The boy is comfortable," the Old Man said. "But we wait for X rays if anything's in his head."

"He's conscious, Papa?" Angelo asked.

"Of course he's conscious. How else would he agree to paint my picture?"

"David says someone hit him, Papa," Rosetta said. "What happened?"

"Your brother knocks on a door," the Old Man said, "and for this the crazy wrought iron hits him. Me, I interrupt the same wrought iron, but for me he goes back through his door to wait for police." The Old Man spread his hands, inviting a conclusion. "Huh!"

"David says you were wonderful, Papa," Gina said.

The Old Man shrugged. "It's a job. Though I'm not sure who pays."

"Can we see Uncle Sal?" Marie asked.

"Of course we can see him," Mama said. "I am his mother."

. . .

When Mama turned into Salvatore's room, she ran to his bedside. "Oh, my poor poor boy in his bandages!"

"Hi, Mama. What, no grapes?"

Mama turned to the children. "Who will get grapes for my Salvatore?"

"No, no, Mama. It was a joke."

"In a hospital and he makes jokes, my son. *My* son in the possessive sense."

"Mama . . . ?"

"Yes, today I met your Heather."

"You . . . met Heather? You saw her?"

"Of course I saw her. How else could she SLURP me and then leave the bottle and a brush? So now I'm fine again, no more worries. And the important thing is my possessive boy recovers."

"Who is Heather, Mum?" Marie asked Gina.

"It's my Salvatore's woman for three months and a week and maybe a day or two," Mama announced. "And, this woman is pregnant."

Suddenly everyone was silent.

"Yes, pregnant!" Mama said.

Eyes turned to the bed.

"Heather told you?" Salvatore said.

"I told her, but she agreed, so it's the same."

"And did she . . . did she tell you . . . that the baby is not mine?"

Eyes widened and turned back to Mama.

"That much I work out for myself. This baby is four months, I think. Or maybe more. Yes? And you are only three, and a week, and a few days."

"And . . . you don't mind?"

"What should I mind? That my Salvatore will have a family?"

"Wait, wait, Mama. That has not been agreed."

"You have a woman. She has a baby. What agreeing? More babies you can make for yourself. Ask your father to explain. Even now he knows how."

Eyes turned to the Old Man.

"Huh."

"Mama," Salvatore said, "I don't even know if Heather wants me to be this baby's father. And it is her decision."

"Of course she wants."

"I know her better than you do, Mama. And she's not like other women."

"I know she's not like. She spits and you feel better."

Salvatore laughed.

Angelo said to Gina, "Do you have any idea at all what they are talking about?"

"Sally's Heather is a saliva therapist."

"A what?"

"Later."

"Speaking of Heather," Salvatore said, "could somebody give her a ring for me?"

"Maybe one day soon you give Heather a ring for yourself," Mama said.

"I meant a—"

"I know what you meant, and I know what I meant." Mama chuckled. Humming, she left the room.

22

*W*ho had the *pla muek paht pick?*" Angelo said.

"Mine." Rosetta took the open container and lifted it to smell. "Mmmmm, good."

"With all the wonderful food that's available to take out on Walcot Street, sometimes I think there's not much point our cooking," Angelo said.

"Oh, yes?" Rosetta said.

"But then I remember how exquisite my sister's cooking is." Angelo's eyes moved around the table. "And my wife's. And my mother's. And I realize that the restaurants are there just so our wonderful cooks don't burn themselves out from overwork."

"I can scramble eggs," David said.

"You can scramble anything," Marie said.

"At least I don't poach things."

"I gave you your tenner. What's the problem?"

Angelo said, "And who had the *mu paht bai*—"

"Mine was pork with basil leaves and chili," Mama said. "Is that *moo pot pie?*"

"There you go, Mama."

As she took the container, Mama said, "Are you sure Salvatore will be all right with just his Heather to hold his hand?"

"Nothing, the X rays showed," the Old Man said.

"They're only keeping him in overnight for observation, Mama," Angelo said. "And Heather's observing him."

"Or licking him." Mama turned to her food.

Gina said, "I've got two cases I need help with. Are people in the mood?"

"What cases? The nine nine nine?" the Old Man said.

"That one's finished, Papa."

"How finished?" the Old Man asked with a frown.

As Angelo distributed the rest of the food, Gina explained about Louis the blip driver and his attempt to please Susan by warning her mother.

"That's so stupid," Marie said. "Why would that make the girl like him?"

David said, "How did Louis get the pager number? Was it by hacking, Mum?"

"No. At the air traffic college they have electronic people who let him play with a scanner."

"Electronic people," Mama said. "My my."

"Louis followed Esta around with this scanner machine until her boyfriend paged her. From that Louis was able to get the pager number."

"He followed Esta waving his machine at her?" Angelo said.

"Nerds do such weird things," Marie said.

"So long as somebody pays," the Old Man said.

Rosetta said, "If it's not the nine nine nine, which case do you want to talk about?"

"Two cases," Gina said. "And they're new. In the first case, there is a daughter in a house—"

"Always trouble," David said.

"Hush," Angelo said.

"And the daughter is behaving very strangely."

"Strangely how?" Mama said.

"It revolves around money, Mama," Gina said. "For some reason this girl—and she's Marie's age—this girl seems willing to go to almost any extremes, as long as it produces money."

"Perhaps the girl is hungry," Mama said. "Is the family poor?"

"The family's not rich," Gina said, "but they're comfortable. They certainly eat well. Could you pass the noodles, please?"

Rosetta passed the noodles.

"The family is healthy and warm. The girl has a room of her own."

"So, what extremes?" the Old Man asked.

"Well," Gina said, "the girl associates with dangerous, criminal people on the nuttiest promises of profit. She meets these people despite the anxiety it causes her family. And she lies to her parents and treats them as if they're stupid."

"Perhaps treatment is needed for this girl," Mama said.

"A psychiatrist, you mean?" Gina asked.

"How about sewage treatment?" David said.

"Or maybe," Mama said, "maybe even Salvatore's nice, pregnant Heather could help with her licking and her brushing and her dips."

"Or Rosetta's Christopher," David said.

"Hush, David," Angelo said.

"The parents are desperate," Gina said. "They're ready to try almost anything."

"They could send her away," the Old Man said. "For such a bad daughter there must be an institution."

"I don't think she is fundamentally bad, Papa," Gina said, "but it all comes back to her foolhardy urge to acquire money."

"Why does she want this money?" Rosetta asked.

"A good question, Rose," Gina said. "An excellent question. Why does she want money so very badly? What do you think? Marie?"

Marie sat grim-faced and silent, elbows by her plate.

"Uncooked joints off the table," David said.

"Marie?" Gina said again.

Marie sat up. "Maybe," she said slowly, "maybe Christmas is coming and this girl likes to give people nice presents."

"You see?" Mama said. "Marie is such a good girl, she thinks only of nice reasons for this daughter to cause heartbreak to her family."

"But you would think," Angelo said, "that in such a situation the daughter would be willing to work for the money, in a proper job."

"She would be only too happy to work," Marie said. "But her parents won't let her have a part-time job because they say it will interfere with her schoolwork, which is a complete crock, by the way."

"Surely," Gina said, "there's a difference between a part-time job all year and a seasonal job."

"But suppose there was a job," Angelo said.

"What job?" Marie asked.

"Suppose, say, a dress shop needed extra help for Christmas. Suppose this girl's parents arranged for her to work there, starting tomorrow morning. What do you think the girl would say?"

"I think she would say, 'Great!' "

"And 'thank you,' she would say too," Mama said, "for such understanding parents."

"Yeah," Marie said, "and thank you."

"But," Angelo said, "wouldn't such a job just be a reward for her bad behavior? How could her parents trust that the girl learned her lesson, that she would become more thoughtful and responsible in the future?"

"I'm sure she would have learned her lesson," Marie said.

"What lesson is that?" Angelo asked.

"That she should talk to her parents about her problems and ask their advice and not think they're too stupid to understand. And that she shouldn't do things that are stupid either."

"What stupid things?" Gina said.

"Mixing with dangerous people."

"And how about other things?" Gina said. "Like starting to smoke? That would be pretty stupid too, wouldn't it?"

"I'm sure she would never do *that,*" Marie said, "even if she had already flirted with it once or twice and was under enormous peer pressure."

"You see," Mama said, "this Marie sees only the nice things in people."

"You said a case," the Old Man said. "There's no case unless somebody is paying."

"There's more than one way to pay, Papa," Gina said.

"Now, the other case has to do with a boy. It's rather puzzling, because he's normally a conscientious student, but recently—" But Gina was interrupted by the telephone.

"It might be the hospital," Mama said.

"I'll get it before I continue." Gina left the table.

"Ah, that reminds me," Angelo said. "David?"

"What, Dad?"

"This afternoon there was a telephone call. A girl, asking for you."

David's eyes opened wide. "When?"

"Not long before you got home."

"What did she say?"

"She said nothing. She wouldn't even leave her name when I asked."

"She didn't say to call back?"

"Without a name or a number?" Angelo said. "Not so easy."

"Oh, Dad!"

"But we might have her voice on the answering machine. It started before I answered."

David jumped out of his seat. He rushed to his mother's side and pointed to himself, asking by gesture if the call was for him.

Gina waved him away. David ran to the office where the answering machine was.

"You mustn't be too hard on him," Marie said to Mama. "He's in love. But he's not a bad boy at heart. He'll settle down in a year or three."

"You see?" Mama said. "Always this Marie sees the good. Even if such a boy as David is too young to settle down.

But . . ." Mama turned to Rosetta. "My Rose, now that's a different story. So when do we meet this handsome undertaker of yours at last? Do we have to die, or will he come to dinner first?"

"He'll come to dinner Sunday, Mama."

"Because that would make me a happy woman."

Gina returned to the table. "It was Charlie."

"He has news about the wrought iron?" the Old Man said. "He has confessed to the uncle?"

"How did you know they suspect him of that, Papa?"

"If the wrought iron is so quick to attack my Salvatore in the head, perhaps he did the same with the uncle when he lived next door."

"Well, as a matter of fact, Charlie says there are officers on their way now to look in a shed at the bottom of Valerie's garden. Simon—the wrought iron—worked in it when he lived at Valerie's. And Charlie says there may well still be a hammer there with Phillip Foxwell's blood on it."

"He does it once, he probably does it twice," the Old Man said.

"And Charlie also says Simon says he's sorry about Salvatore."

"Sorry?" Mama said. "He's *sorry?*"

"Yes, Mama."

"For what he did to my Salvatore he should go to jail without a key."

Angelo asked, "Are they going to release Winston?"

"They're still questioning him about his so-called lottery money."

"Why 'so-called'?"

"Charlie says Winston probably found it somewhere in the house. The police think it is probably proceeds from Phillip Foxwell's fencing activities."

"Who cares," the Old Man said, "so long as somebody pays."

"Well, I think Winston's wife will care. Winston may be safer staying in jail," Gina said. "But at least the police will be dropping the murder charges."

"For Simon the wrought iron to pick up," the Old Man said.

"You know, Papa," Angelo said, "I think the court might just decide that Simon the wrought iron is deranged."

"If the reason he hits is for no good reason," the Old Man said, "that's deranged. Crazy even. Huh!"

"And you know what that would mean, don't you?"

"What?"

"He would get manslaughter by reason of diminished responsibility. And that means it wouldn't be a murder, Papa."

"Not a murder?"

"You would still have solved the agency's only murder."

"Ah," the Old Man said. "Now Norman Stiles, *there* was murder."

Everyone else at the table moaned.